A Window to the World

Eunice Boeye

PublishAmerica
Baltimore

First printing

ISBN: 1-4137-3212-7
PUBLISHED BY PUBLISHAMERICA, LLLP
www.publishamerica.com
Baltimore

Printed in the United States of America

To my children: Kathy, Kandy, Kelly, and Ronnie.
And to my granddaughter, Jordyn, who shares a
birthday with Annie

I am indebted to Dr. Ken Carvell of Morgantown, who walked with my daughter, Kandy Boeve, and me one beautiful October day in those golden woods of West Virginia and shared with us his considerable knowledge of the area. I also owe Vicki Constable, Sharon Krafft, and my daughter, Kathy Boeve-Pensabene—special thanks for reading my story with sharp eyes and gentle critiques.

Chapter One

Blossom and the Rock Ledge

He appeared before us as suddenly as though he'd dropped down to the forest floor on a golden shaft of October sunlight. He was an old man with long, white whiskers and ragged clothes, and he was leading Blossom.

"Reckon this old bossy-cow be yourn." There was a kindness to the old man's voice, a twinkle in his pale blue eyes. "Reckon one of ya be James Duncan's girl. Heard he be off somewheres to California."

"I'm Annie Duncan," I said, "and that cow is ours. Her name is Blossom. We've been looking for her all afternoon." I took a deep breath and added, although I didn't know it to be true, "Pa's still in California."

The old man gave me a somber nod and his gaze shifted from me to Johanna.

"Ya ain't a Duncan…don't look to be one, anyway."

I introduced Johanna, adding, "She's my friend."

"A Haskell, huh?" Eyes squinted, the old man studied Johanna. "Don't rightly know the Haskell name. Knowed ya someone else's girl, though, being so pale-skinned and all."

Johanna gave him a timid smile and fingered her long, blonde hair, a nervous habit of hers.

The old man's gaze shifted back to me. "Knowed right off ya was a Duncan. Favor your pa, ya do, 'ceptin' for that mess of freckles." The old man's sudden smile, almost lost in his scraggly beard, was warm as sunshine and so engaging that I could not help but smile back at him. There had been no sting in his remark about my freckles, and I knew he'd meant no offense.

"I 'spect you all be wonderin' why I's needin' your cow." As he spoke, he scratched vigorously at his side.

I nodded, wondering if he had fleas. That thought brought little itches popping up under my brown linsey wool dress, and I could almost see them leap from the old man into my head of curly, reddish-brown hair. I squirmed a little, but kept my hands still, holding tight to the coil of short rope I'd brought for Blossom.

"Got me some un'spected company and my larder ain't never near big enough to feed more'n me," the old man went on, his right hand going suddenly behind him to scratch at a new itch on his backside. "Was out gettin' me a turkey to feed 'em and came 'cross bossy here. Knowed her to be James Duncan's, and knowed he ain't gonna mind if'n I borryed her, 'counta her milk be good for the young'un." He turned to untie the rope around Blossom's neck. I noticed that he had tied up the clapper of her bell. His eyes darted from my face to Blossom's bell and back again. "I tied it up on 'counta it makin' such a din. Do ya want I should untie it?"

I shook my head. Thoughts of the old man's "unexpected

guests" had made me a little jumpy, and I sure didn't need the noise of Blossom's bell to announce our presence on the way out of these woods.

"Since I ain't gonna be needin' her no more—my guests done gone—I's bringin' her home to ya." He nodded at the rope I held in my hand. "Want me to put it on fer ya?"

I had smelled a bad odor when the old man first appeared before us on the trail. As I stepped up close to hand him the rope, I nearly gagged. I had to force myself not to step back for I didn't want to appear rude or frightened of him. Even though he smelled like he never bathed and the clothes on his skinny frame were tattered and encrusted with grime, his baggy pants held up with a piece of twine, his white hair and beard wild and uncombed, and he probably had fleas, I wasn't afraid of him. He had such a gentle smile and such warm blue eyes, I felt I could have trusted him with my life.

"I do be thankin' ya, Missy," the old man said as I reached for the end of the rope he held out to me. I imagined fleas crawling from him down the rope to my hand and it was all I could do to take hold of my end.

With a small bow towards me and another towards Johanna, he turned and patted Blossom's side. "I'm a-thankin' ya, too, bossy-girl." He looked back at us again, smiled, and stepped off the faint deer trail, into the trees, and was gone.

"Who was that?" Johanna asked, her blue eyes wide.

"I don't know," I said. "Someone who lives back up in these hills, I guess. Someone who knows my pa." I wrinkled my nose, remembering his smell. "Someone not used to soap and water, that's for sure."

Johanna grinned. "He sure scratched a lot." Her face suddenly sobered and a puzzled frown appeared. "I wonder who his unexpected guests were?"

I shivered and cast a quick glance around, certain I knew who the old man had fed with the turkey and Blossom's milk. "I bet they were those runaway slaves your pa heard about in town yesterday."

"But Pa said they were seen over by Morgantown." A shaft of sunlight shining through the trees fell across Johanna's face, and she stepped back under a sweet birch tree. "Even your ma said they weren't likely to come this way."

"I know. They should have gone straight on north from there." I thought about that for a moment and then said, "Maybe they ran onto somebody who would have turned them in, like slave catchers. So instead of going north they angled off this way to keep from getting caught. They were probably already gone from Morgantown when your pa heard about them." I paused, my eyes on Blossom grazing on the sparse grass growing alongside the trail. I turned back to look at Johanna. "We don't know where that old man lives, either. Maybe it's quite a ways back north of here."

Johanna nodded. "Remember he was out hunting for a turkey to feed his guests when he came upon Blossom, so he might have had to take her back several miles to wherever he lives. He'd need a bucket or something for the milk. But whatever happened, let's get on home, before some other smelly old man comes out of these woods." The little grin that had appeared on her face slipped away as she suddenly jerked around to look behind her. "I thought I heard something," she whispered.

A prickling of ghostly fingers danced along my scalp and goose bumps that felt as big as hen eggs rose up on my arms. A squirrel ran up a nearby tree, chattering. *Had someone or something frightened it?* I pulled on Blossom's rope. She swung her big head up and eyed me, her jaws working rhythmically. "Come, boss," I coaxed. Blossom stretched out her neck and snapped off another tuft of grass.

Johanna, who had hurried on ahead, stopped to wait for us. Plainly annoyed and more than a little fearful, she raised a beckoning hand. "Hurry up!" she mouthed silently.

Just as annoyed and some scared myself, I walked around Blossom and whacked the flat of my hand on her broad rump. She leaped forward, pulling the rope from my hand. Breaking into a trot, she soon caught up with Johanna who grabbed her rope and held it for me. This time as we started back along the way we had come, Blossom followed along without her usual stubbornness.

As we hurried along, I listened for other sounds besides the chattering of squirrels, the varied bird songs, and the whisper of the paper dry leaves underfoot. But hearing nothing unusual, my fears faded. I loved the forest and had never before felt any fear. Wild animals lived back up in the hills, but I knew they would stay far out of our way, as afraid of us as we would be of them. I had walked alone in these woods before, enjoying the sights and sounds, and I had never been afraid. But meeting the old man and hearing of his unexpected guests had, for a while, made me a little uneasy.

I thought back to when Patrick had come in from milking. "Guess who's gone again?" he said. Ma and I knew immediately, and we both answered, "Blossom." We had just sold her latest calf, a bull calf, all red like her, and when she didn't have a calf to hold her, she would wander off. Sometimes she would put a number of miles between herself and home. Goodness knows where the old man had found her while out hunting for a turkey for his guests. Guests, I was certain, with dark faces. Maybe even a family. He had mentioned a child— a "young'un," he'd said. If he had fed fugitive slaves, then one had been a child. I had never before thought about those slave people running and hiding with their children. It would be so hard, especially with a small child or a baby. I thought of my little brother. Jackson was only six, but he was a tough little boy. He could probably keep up, but Johanna's blonde-haired little sisters with their short, chubby legs would have to be carried most of the way. At two and four, they would not fully understand why they had to run and why they could not be allowed to make a sound. They would be fearful, too, and wanting to cry. I could almost see their big blue eyes filled with silent tears.

What if Johanna and I were slaves? What a different life we would be living, and at twelve we were past old enough, by slave owner standards, to be sold off from our parents. It was likely, too, that I would not even have known my brothers or Johanna, her little sisters. A few months ago, a sale bill tacked beside the livery stable door had advertised two girls for sale; one had been twelve, like Johanna and me. The other had been just ten. They would make good house slaves, the sale bill read. There was no mention of any other slave, no woman of the age to be their mother, and I'd wondered then if they were being sold away from her, and perhaps from their father, too. I hoped if they were sisters or even best friends that they would be sold to the same slave owner. Ma saw me reading the sign and said, "Come on, Annie, there's nothing you can do."

It made me sad to think about those girls. I could not imagine life without my mother, especially now that Pa was gone so far away. It would be hard to be separated from Patrick and Jackson, too, and even a best friend. Although I didn't have a sister, I sort of knew, because of Johanna, what it would be like to have one.

I blinked away a gathering mist of tears and tried to put those thoughts out of my mind. Ahead of me, Johanna was almost running, her long, straight, pale gold hair bouncing with each hurried step. I grinned to myself, thinking of the first time I met her.

She had moved here from Minnesota with her family two years ago. Her first day at school it had poured rain all morning, stopping about noon. When we went out for last recess, there were puddles all over the schoolyard, and Johanna, running in a game of tag, fell with a splat into one of them. Plainly embarrassed, her lips had quivered a little, but she'd held on to her tears. I had admired her for that and for ignoring Ben Gilly, who teased her about wallowing like a pig in the mud and whispered "oinking" sounds at her until Miss McKinley heard him and made him stand in the corner.

I didn't know then that Johanna only lived a little over a mile from our place and I was surprised when, after school, she began to walk along our road. I ran to catch up with her. Before we reached the fork in the road, one way leading to our farm and the other to hers, we had become friends.

Saturday afternoons we usually spent together, either at her house or mine. This Saturday, we had planned to alter a dress I'd outgrown, but instead Ma sent us out to look for Blossom.

Remembering those fugitive slaves near Morgantown that Johanna's pa had heard about, I said to Ma, "What if we see those runaway slaves?"

Ma snapped at me, cross as a hungry old bear coming out of hibernation. "Morgantown's over ten miles due west of here," she said. 'Unless they're fools, they went on straight north. Besides," she'd added, "they sure won't be a chasing around in broad daylight showing themselves to a couple of twelve-year-old girls."

Outside I'd apologized to Johanna for the sharpness of Ma's voice. "She's worried near to death about Pa. Patrick went to Burns Ferry this morning, and if there's no letter waiting this time, Ma's going to be really upset."

Thoughts of Pa had shadowed our days ever since he left for the California gold fields last February. I often wished that gold had never been discovered near that place called Sutter's Fort in January of 1848, or at least hadn't lured our pa away. Like Pa, a lot of folks had not been able to resist the chance of becoming rich. Even now, two years later, there's still folks either planning to go or have just recently pulled up stakes. The gold fever has slowed some, now that a few folks are returning with hard luck stories and no gold to amount to anything. But there will always be those who think they'll be the lucky ones and hit a big strike.

All those folks who left for California last year were called Forty-niners. Pa didn't leave until this year of 1850, so I wasn't sure if he would be called a Forty-niner or not.

My, but he had been excited. The first mention of it and he was ready to sell the farm and take us all west in a covered wagon. But Ma hadn't taken to the idea at all. Pa had tried to change her mind, but she wouldn't budge. She wasn't going to go and that was that. So Pa had gone without us, riding away on Big Jake that cold, cloudy February day. At Burns Ferry, he was to join up with some other men, going as he was without family. As he rode off that frosty morning on his blue roan and leading Samson, Patrick's little sorrel that he was using for a pack horse, I held out hope that he would change his mind and come back home. But my hope died with his first letter. From that letter, posted at Independence, Missouri, we knew he was having the time of his life. His second letter, written at a place called Blue River in Kansas Territory, took sixty days to reach us. It, too, was full of the road he had traveled and the people he'd met. His third and, so far, last letter was posted from an army fort called Kearny. It is in Indian territory, but Pa reported the Indians to be friendly, which was certainly a relief. He promised another letter at a place called Fort Bridger, but we've never received it.

Although there seemed to be few problems with Indians, the folks coming back tell of accidents and illnesses, especially the dreaded cholera, which is almost always fatal, so we can't help but worry about Pa.

Since Ma never went to school, Patrick writes our letters to Pa, addressing them to him at Sutter's Fort in California. Mr. McDaniels sends them from his store and post office at Burns Ferry by stage to Independence, Missouri. There, either a traveler takes them on, or they're sent with the US Army, who sends men back and forth from their forts out west. The army, or folks coming back who have given up on their dream of riches, for one reason or another, bring letters back with them, at least as far as Independence. Usually then, they go on by stage. Patrick says there are ships sailing from California that also carry mail.

Every time we go into Burns Ferry, we stop first at Mr. McDaniels's store and post office to see if we have a letter from Pa. I sure hoped there would be one there today. In my imagination, I see Patrick pull Nick and Ned up to the hitching post, jump from the wagon, and step up on the boardwalk and into the store. I see Mr. McDaniels look up, smile a big smile, and hobble back to the nest of letter boxes for Pa's letter. I think if I can just imagine it clear enough, it will come true.

When Pa first left, my daydreams always brought him home with pockets and saddlebags filled with gold. I imagined all the wonderful things we would buy: fine clothes, a big, new house... Pa would no longer plow the fields and the horses could grow fat and lazy—and every day I would take them sugar loaves to nibble. But I didn't care about those things anymore. Now, I just wanted to know that Pa was safe; and I wanted him home.

Blossom insisted on stopping to drink at a small stream trickling down from the hillside. This time we waited patiently. Johanna's fears, like mine, had given way to rational thought. "That old man could have fed a family of white folks passing through," she offered.

I agreed, although I wondered why they wouldn't be traveling the roads.

While we waited, I looked up at the hills above us and noticed a slab of black rock jutting out from the hillside. I turned to Johanna in a rush of excitement. "Look, up there. See? Jutting out from the side of the hill? I'm sure that's one of those overhanging slabs of rock Pa told me about. He said that in the early days, the Indians used to make their camps under those rocks, not only for shelter, but also for protection from enemies."

I did not notice if Johanna answered me, for a memory had come to me with a little spurt of anger. I was nine or ten years old, and Pa, talking about seeing a rock ledge shelter that day, had promised he'd take me to see it. I wondered if it was this one that he'd found. If it was, it probably wasn't more than five miles from our farm. *It wouldn't have taken much time or effort for him to bring me here.*

We have a lot of black rock of all sizes here in western Virginia. Often we see the large boulder-sized ones in jumbled piles with some scattered about. I always think it looks as if a giant baby has been playing with them and then left to play with something else. This slab of rock on the hillside above us was a huge overhang, maybe not quite half the size of the roof of our house. It would be well hidden in summer when the trees and bushes around it were thick with leaves. Now, in late October, most of the leaves had fallen and lay scattered on the forest floor, and only the laurel was still green. If it were some other time, I would have climbed the hill to see what it was like beneath that slab of black rock, but not today. It was getting late and Patrick should be home soon.

After Blossom drank her fill, we hurried on, the image of the rock ledge in my mind. Some day, I wanted to go back there.

As we came out onto the road leading to our farm and could walk side by side, I said to Johanna, "I wouldn't mind going back to that rock ledge some day and looking around."

Johanna frowned. "There might be snakes."

"Maybe. Maybe not," I said. Johanna wasn't much of an outdoor girl. She could get scared at just the thought of snakes and other wild creatures. I've always told her that they left you alone if you left them alone, but she finds that hard to believe.

"We could come back in the spring with a picnic lunch," I said.

A small grin touched Johanna's lips. "Only if Blossom runs away again, and she runs this way, and we have to look for her. Otherwise, I'm not going back there."

"Okay," I said, no longer caring about the rock ledge, for the roof of the barn had come into view and my thoughts had raced on home, anxious and eager, even as my heart stilled with a cold touch of fear. Was Patrick back from Burns Ferry, yet? This time, had he brought a letter from Pa? Or would we never ever hear from our pa again?

Chapter Two

The Letter

It was near suppertime when Patrick got home. Jackson, playing outside, heard the horses and the jingle of the harnesses and called out to us before running up the road to meet him. Patrick drove the team up into the yard. He had stopped for Jackson to climb up on the seat beside him. There was no need for words. Patrick's somber face and the tear-smeared dirt on Jackson's told us all there was to say. I had to struggle to hold back my tears.

If only Pa had not gone to California, or if Ma hadn't been so stubborn. "I'm not about to go off into some wilderness on the strength of some fool pipe dream," she'd said. Once Ma got her back up, she could be as unmovable as that big rock ledge back along the trail. Pa was just as stubborn, and he had his heart just as set on going as Ma's was on staying home. So when he met some other men not taking their families, he'd gone with them. I know Patrick hated it that Pa took Samson, his little sorrel, for a packhorse. Of course, our workhorses, Nick and Ned, were needed to pull the plow and our wagon, so he couldn't take them. Patrick had raised Samson from a colt, and the horse followed him about like a pet dog. I wondered if the horse missed Patrick as much as I was sure Patrick missed him.

After Pa left, I started to understand that those exciting headlines in the newspapers and all that talk about California being a fair, golden land, where, it was said, nuggets as big as goose eggs could be found, had just been too much for Pa's itchy feet. I knew now that Pa had a thirst for wandering. A thirst that was too great to resist the lure of this new, wonderful land. I thought about those times when Pa would talk about some land somewhere, usually west, maybe Illinois or Missouri, and Ma would get all cranky, and if she talked to us at all, would nearly bite our heads off. When Pa began talking about California and us going with him, she got as worked up as a swarm of angry hornets. One day I heard her tell Pa that Jackson was too young for such a long journey. "But, Mary, he's five years old," Pa said.

Ma's eyes had flashed with fire. "He's still awfully young," she snapped, and said something else about the twins. Something I didn't quite understand. Pa's face turned white as our good Sunday plates. It was a long time before he mentioned California again.

Whatever Ma said about the twins sure had me confused. It sounded like she thought it was Pa's fault that those babies died on our way here from our old farm back in New York.

I tried to figure it out by going back in my mind to that rainy day when we arrived here at what was to become our new farm. The babies, twin girls we'd named Sarah and Martha, had been coughing and feverish for days. When we got close to our new land, instead of turning off, Ma insisted that Pa drive us on into the town, which was Burns Ferry. "And hope, by all that is good and holy," she said, "there will be a doctor there." There was.

Dr. Isaac. But he couldn't save our babies. The sight of my mother clutching those little bodies, her tears falling like the rain streaming down outside the doctor's little office, still lived as clear as spring water in my memory. *What,* I wondered, *could Pa have possibly done to make him look so guilty and turn his face so white?*

Pa didn't say anymore about California for a month or two, and I had half forgotten about it when I heard them arguing again. This time Ma reminded Pa that Patrick was to apprentice to a lawyer friend of Dr. Isaac's in Pittsburgh to learn the law.

Pa thought Patrick, at sixteen, was old enough to leave behind. "Later, after his studies," he said, "he can join us in California."

Ma's eyes got dark as storm clouds, and she yelled that she wasn't leaving any of her family behind. Not even for a year or two. Not ever!

Then Pa asked why Patrick couldn't apprentice out to a lawyer in California.

To that, Ma said, she doubted there'd be a single lawyer out in California tending to their law business. "They'll be as gold-crazy as the rest of you fools and out digging or whatever you do, like everybody else."

Pa ignored the fool part. "All right, then," he said. "There's a group of single men going. I'll go with them."

I'd wanted to say, "Don't go, Pa. Please, don't leave us." But I never said the words.

I think a part of me knew he'd go anyway.

Pa said Patrick could work the farm until he got back and then they'd send him off to a big college to learn the law. "I'll have the money then," he said.

"If you find any gold." Ma retorted. "I don't expect it's just laying around waiting for someone to pick it up." She turned from where she was working some bread dough on a floured board, slapping the soft lump of dough around, so even if you didn't see her eyes blazing with anger, you still knew she was mad. "If it's as easy as that to find, it'll be long gone before you get there."

I always wondered if it was as much Ma's wish as Patrick's to become a lawyer. Maybe she was wishing she could have been a man so she could have become a lawyer herself. For it seemed to me they both talked of it together. Of course, Ma had never had any schooling at all. She couldn't read or write more than her name. Patrick fairly soaked up learning. Miss McKinley came to teach when Patrick was still in school, and she boarded some at our home. She told Ma she sure had a time keeping ahead of Patrick.

I wondered if Ma would have been as quick to learn if her pa hadn't thought that school was wasted on girls. I was sure she was every bit as smart as Patrick. I always thought that if Ma was younger or Patrick older, they'd pass for twins. They were both bone thin with blue eyes that turned black when they were angry, and both had the same straight-as-a-string black hair.

Like the smelly old man in the woods had said, I favored Pa, although I supposed I would never be nearly as tall. But, like Pa, I was stockily built and had the same brown eyes and curly, reddish-brown hair. Before I was old enough to comb out my own tangles, Ma used to say my hair was "as thick as a bear's winter coat." Sometimes, working a brush and comb through it, I thought so, too. Jackson didn't look so much like any one of us. His eyes were brown, but lighter than mine and Pa's, more of a hazel shade, and his hair was bright red. I was the only one with freckles. Like that old man said, I had a mess of them. Pa always called those reddish-brown specks all over my face and arms "cinnamon spots." Just thinking about how he used to take me on his lap when I was little and trace his big fingers from spot to spot made my eyes well up with tears. He usually counted to fifty or a hundred and then he'd jump the number to the thousands or millions. He always said my freckles lent spice to my face and made me special. When he first left, I missed him dearly. But then I had expected to see him again. Now, the fear that something had happened to him made a cold, empty place in my heart.

Ma was surprised when I told her about the old man who had "borryed" Blossom. She didn't know him and neither did Patrick.

"How would he have known Pa?" I asked.

"You know how your Pa would take off every now and then and go back up into the hills for few days," Ma said. "He always said he needed 'breathing room.' Perhaps he met that old fella on one of those jaunts of his."

I thought she was probably right.

Both Ma and Patrick suspected, like Johanna and I did, that the old man's unexpected guests had been those runaways seen over by Morgantown.

When Dr. Isaac came by to see us, as he often did, having become our dearest friend and like a grandfather to me and Patrick and Jackson, he said, "Sounds like old Looney Barnes. He's a good old fella, would give you the shirt off his back, but," he grinned, "it would be so dirty and probably so flea infested you wouldn't want it."

I laughed. "He kept scratching the whole time he talked to us."

Dr. Isaac smiled at me. "If his guests were fugitive slaves," he said, "it must have been about too much to be running and hiding, and when they did find a friendly face—to have to hold their noses. He smells bad enough, but his shack would rival a ripe carcass." He looked at Ma and his face sobered. "I went there once with James to treat the old fella for the ague. James heated some water and we gave him a bath and washed his clothes and bedding and aired the place out." He paused and grinned, "Figured it would either kill or cure him." He shook his head. "If his guests were those runaways, even half-starved, I'll bet their bellies lurched a bit getting the food down."

We didn't hear any more about runaway slaves; and Patrick took to staking Blossom out on a long rope, sending Jackson out a couple of times a day to be sure she hadn't tangled herself up in it.

The next Sunday, Patrick drove us to church as he has each Sunday since Pa went west. Johanna had been sick for a week and had missed school. I was so happy to see her in the wagon with her family as they pulled up into the churchyard. But we didn't get a chance to talk as we had to go right into church. Dr. Isaac, who came most Sundays, was absent. "He must have been called to tend someone," Ma said.

Already a cloudy morning, during church the clouds had darkened and grown heavy with the threat of rain, so everyone was anxious to get home. Johanna and I didn't have a moment to visit. We both looked forward to school tomorrow and walking home afterwards.

Monday was cold with a brisk north wind. After school, Johanna and I drew our mufflers up about our faces and hurried towards our homes, glad to be facing away from the wind. I thought about those runaways Johanna's pa had heard about, and I said to Johanna that I sure hoped they were some place safe and warm, especially if they had a little child with them.

"I wonder if that old man did help them." Johanna's eyes twinkled and she gave a little laugh. "If he did, they probably hope they don't run across any more like him."

"It's better than getting caught and going back to being a slave," I said.

Her face sobering, Johanna said, "You're right." A small frown wrinkled her brow. "Can you imagine owning a slave, Annie?"

"No," I said, and told her it was probably because we came from places where people didn't own slaves. Johanna's family, before they moved here, had lived in Minnesota. We had come here from New York State. "Patrick says if you've grown up owning slaves, it likely seems a perfectly normal way of life."

"I imagine he's right." Johanna pushed a strand of blonde hair back in under her hood. "Anyway, I'm glad we don't have many slaves here in this part of Virginia."

"Patrick says we'd have them if we had big plantations like they do in the east and farther south, but our small hill farms aren't conducive to slavery."

Johanna's eyes again twinkled merrily above her cold, reddened cheeks. "Conducive! You do get some awful big words from your brother, don't you?"

I laughed. "You know how Miss McKinley is always saying we should work everyday on building our vocabulary. It's not hard for me, I just listen to Patrick."

Johanna grinned. "Lucky you," she said.

When we parted where a well-worn footpath angled off towards Johanna's, I began to run, thinking of the warm fire at home. As I came in sight of the house, I saw Dr. Isaac's black buggy pulled up to the gate. It was late in the day for visiting, so he must have been on a call that brought him by here on his way home. If he came anywhere near our place, he always stopped to see us, if only for a few minutes.

Patrick, coming up from the barn, met me at the gate where Dr. Isaac's small brown mare waited. Brownie turned her head to look past her blinders as we walked up beside her. I pulled off a mitten and rubbed my hand along her neck.

"Did Dr. Isaac just get here?" I asked Patrick.

He nodded, a frown wrinkling his forehead. "He called to me to come up to the house, which is unusual since he knows I'd come anyway." A whisper of alarm coursed through me as, his frown deepening, he added, "There was something in his voice that disturbed me."

Patrick pushed open the door and I followed him into the warmth of the kitchen. My first thought was that everything must be fine. They sat at the table, Dr. Isaac and Ma, with Jackson on Dr. Isaac's lap. The smell of fresh baked bread filled the room, reminding me I was hungry. But all thoughts of food vanished when I saw the stiff, scared look on Ma's face.

"Annie. I'm glad you're here, too." Dr. Isaac got to his feet, setting Jackson off his lap, but keeping an arm around him. He picked up a square of light tan paper from the table.

"This letter came today," he said. "It's from out west, but it's not your pa's handwriting."

I sucked in my breath, fear clutching me in a cold, tight grip, and looked at Ma. She swallowed hard before speaking, but her voice still came out weak and trembling. "I wanted to wait for you two," she said.

Dr. Isaac turned the letter over in his hand. "Jeb McDaniels closed up his store to bring it to me. He said he'd of brought it out himself if I hadn't been home. He's so stove up with rheumatism, everything is an effort for him. He'll have to give up that store before long." He shook his head. "Sorry," he said. "I'm rambling."

He motioned Patrick and me to the table. Patrick sat down across from Ma and pulled Jackson up on his lap. I slipped onto a chair beside him. Towser, our old, black dog, rose up from his warm place behind the stove, and wagging his tail, came to stand beside Patrick and Jackson's chair. Jackson reached out to the dog and the filmy, old eyes closed with pleasure at the touch of his small hand. Old Towser had always been Pa's dog, but now, with Pa gone, he seemed to favor Jackson.

Dr. Isaac cleared his throat, broke the seal, and unfolded the letter. "It's from Clement Richards," he said.

We all knew he was one of the men who had left with Pa last February. My eyes blurred and I felt suddenly dizzy. I shook my head and my vision cleared, the dizziness fading.

"Dear Mrs. Duncan," Dr. Isaac began, " I write this letter with a heavy heart for you and the children."

My heart lurched inside my chest.

"Your husband, James," Dr. Isaac's voice roughened, "is missing, ma'am, and most likely no longer in the land of the living." He paused, his eyes seeking Ma's.

"Go on," she said, her voice, like her face, had turned as cold and bleak as winter's wind.

My ears could not take in all the words Dr. Isaac read from that sheet of paper. The dizziness came back to swirl inside my head and my ears caught only scraps of the words. "We was sick as dogs. Maddox, Rice, and Heap died. Your James and me, we was gettin' some better, but we was needin' meat bad.

Your James went to shoot us some. Rode up into the hills… He never did come back."

My eyes grew heavy with tears and my heart felt like it had broken into pieces. Patrick pulled Jackson's head up against his shoulder, one hand cupping the little boy's red head of hair, the other he closed over my hand. At first the warmth of his hand was comforting, then his grip tightened, hurting me, and I pulled away. Patrick lifted the hand that had held mine and wiped the corners of his eyes.

The letter read, Dr. Isaac refolded it and sat down again, heavily, as if his legs could no longer hold him. A silence filled up the room and beat against my eardrums.

Ma was the first to move. Pushing up out of her chair, she grabbed her old, black shawl, and went outside. A chill from the opened door touched me with icy fingers.

Jackson slid from Patrick's lap to the floor and hid his tear-streaked face in Towser's warm black coat. Patrick went to the window and looked out. Turning back, he said to Dr. Isaac, "She's going up to the twins' grave. Should I go with her?"

"No. She needs some time alone," Dr. Isaac said. The full weight of his seventy years sounded in his voice and fear coursed through me. I had never before thought of him as old. Would we soon lose him, too? Blinded by a flood of tears, I stumbled to my room, and flinging myself across my bed, cried until I could cry no more.

Chapter Three

Towser

I slept and woke to cry again. Each time I slept, the dreams came. Dark and frightening, they brought me up out of sleep, trembling with fear. Finally, too afraid to shut my eyes and let those awful dreams come again, I spent the rest of the night staring into the inky darkness of my small room.

Dr. Isaac stayed with us, sleeping in the loft with Patrick and Jackson. He left the next morning, stopping at the Haskell's to give them the sad news. Mrs. Haskell and Johanna called in the late afternoon, bringing a hot dish of ham and potatoes for our supper. I met them at the door, explaining to Mrs. Haskell that Ma was in bed and had been there all day.

"It's been a blow to her… to all of you," Mrs. Haskell said with a gentle smile, her blue eyes warm with sympathy. "Maybe she'll get up and eat a bite. If not, you children be sure to eat. You need to keep up your strength."

I was sure Ma would be up the next day. Even when she was sick, she never stayed overlong in bed. "There's too much to do to lie abed," she often said when Pa tried to get her to rest. Even when she was really sick and looked like "death warmed over," as Pa always said, she went about her work. But this time she stayed in bed all day and the next day, too. That day turned into another and another, and still she made no effort to leave her bed, except to squat on the slop jar, which, if I hadn't emptied each day would have set there smelling, and I doubt if she'd have cared. At mealtimes, I brought her a plate of food, but she barely touched it. Sometimes she drank a little water, sometimes nibbled at a piece of bread, or took a small bite of potato, but she never ate enough to give herself any strength. Her dark hair, pulled from its usual bun at the nape of her neck, became matted and tangled and the shadows that grew under her eyes turned dark as bruises. Everyday I grew more afraid. If she didn't get out of bed soon, I was sure she would waste away and die.

A week passed and Dr. Isaac came to see us, apologizing for not coming sooner, but there was a lot of sickness going around that had kept him away tending to other folks. He was in Ma's room a long while. When he came out, he looked at us and shook his head.

"What'll we do?" Patrick asked. His eyes darkened, and for a moment, fear looked out of them.

"I don't know." Dr. Isaac sank down in a chair. The wrinkles in his face looked deep as plowed furrows. "I'll talk to Mrs. Haskell, maybe she can help."

The next morning, Mrs. Haskell and Johanna came with the little girls and stayed the day. I had supper almost ready, Johanna helping me, when Mrs. Haskell brought Ma out of her bedroom and sat her down at the table. Ma's matted and tangled hair was pulled back again into a bun, but not the smooth glossy one she usually wore, and a straggle of dark strands hung loose about her neck. Leaving Ma at the table, where she sat staring listlessly at her hands folded in front of her, Mrs. Haskell carried Ma's bedding out to the clothesline to air and asked Patrick to carry in several pails of water to heat on the stove. After Mrs. Haskell got a few bites of supper into Ma, she had Patrick bring in the tub and hang the privacy curtain. Ignoring Ma's protests, Mrs. Haskell made her bathe, and afterwards helped her into a clean nightgown and back into her freshly aired bed.

Every morning, Mrs. Haskell came to get Ma out of bed and eating a few bites. I didn't know when she got her back to being her old self again, for one morning I woke with a sore throat and a fever that lasted well past a week and mostly stayed in bed myself. Sometime during that week, Ma got up and went about her work again.

A bubble of laughter brought me up out of sleep the morning I was to go back to school. The laughter was my own, brought on by a dream that I was riding behind Pa on Big Jake, his blue roan horse. Up hills and down into valleys we rode, my arms clinging to Pa's waist, my laughter floating back on the wind. But as I came fully awake and realized it had been just a dream, my laughter dissolved into tears. Through wet, blurry eyes, I looked toward the frost-coated window of my room and my thoughts went back to that June day when Pa had finished putting in the window in this room he had built on to the back of the house just for me. I was helping Ma in the kitchen when Pa called for me. Ma came behind me, drying her hands on her apron.

A big grin on his face, Pa opened the window wide and the sun-warmed air blew through on a soft breeze. "Miss, Duncan," he said, with a sweeping flourish of his hand. "Your very own window to the world."

"Oh thank you, Pa." I went to the window and looked out at

the trees behind the house.

He came up behind me and put his hands on my shoulders. "When you look out this window, Annie," he said, "think about what lies beyond these hills of Virginia."

Behind us Ma said, her voice sharp-edged as Pa's skinning knife, "James! Don't go putting fool notions in the child's head."

I wondered at it then, but now, I knew. Ma had been afraid he was getting restless and wanting to move on again.

Knowing I'd be late for school if I didn't get up very soon, I flipped back the covers. Shivering as my bare feet touched the cold floor, a sudden thought struck me. *Had Ma, that day, also worried that Pa was trying to influence me, to get me to want to move on, too?*

Miss McKinley was ringing the last bell as I came in sight of the school, and I had to run the last few yards not to be late. Hanging my cloak on a hook in the outer hallway, I took my seat at the end of the bench where I always sat with Johanna. But this morning, she wasn't there. Later in the morning, I asked Miss McKinley and she told me Johanna's mother was ill and needed her daughter at home.

I hoped Johanna's mother wasn't very sick and would soon be well again. I wondered if Ma would go see her and help her out, like she had helped Ma. By the time school was out, I had decided to stop by Johanna's, so I could let Ma know if Mrs. Haskell needed her.

The Haskells have always had a lot of dogs, and as I came in sight of Johanna's house, they all came running to greet me. I had gotten into the habit of counting them. When there are puppies, there's often as many as ten. Today there were just five, all familiar to me but one small tan-colored one. They crowded against me as they always did, the small tan one just as eager to be petted as the others. They were always friendly to me, but Johanna said a stranger coming on to the place sure raised their hackles.

Johanna met me at the door. "Oh, Annie," she cried, her hands reached for my mitten-covered ones and drew me inside and over to the warmth of the fireplace. Her two little blonde-haired sisters sat near the hearth engrossed in playing with their rag dolls.

I asked about her mother as I handed my wrap to Johanna. "She has to stay in bed almost all day." Johanna lowered her voice, with a quick look at her little sisters. "Every time she gets out of bed, she throws up. The only things she can keep down, at all, are soda biscuits and a little tea."

Realizing Johanna did not want her little sisters to worry about their ma, I started talking about my day at school. Johanna was eager to know what all we were studying and the half hour I planned to stay went by before we hardly knew it.

At the door, as I was ready to leave, I asked about the small tan-colored dog. "Oh, he just showed up here one day. So I guess he's ours," Johanna said, adding with a small shrug, "unless someone shows up to claim him."

The sky had promised snow all afternoon, and as I came in sight of our farm, big flakes began to fall. Through the thick falling snow, I saw Ma down by the barn. Jackson was huddled close to her, his face pressed against her work coat. Something dark lay at her feet. I quickened my pace, my eyes trying to make sense of what I was seeing. I saw Patrick step out the back door of the house and he was carrying his gun. *His gun!*

I broke into a run, seeing as I came close that the dark shape on the ground was Towser. Horrified, I watched his body shake with spasms, his legs jerk and twitch.

Sick with dread, I looked up at Ma.

Her voice soft, she said, "He just took to having these spells, Annie. He's old and nearly blind. Patrick's bringing the gun to put him out of his misery. We can't save him."

"But he was Pa's dog," I whispered.

"I know," Ma said. "I know."

Chapter Four

Old Bug-Eyes

We had not been to church since the letter about Pa. Reverend Paully had been by for a visit, but he was very understanding and said only, "We hope you and your family will come to church just as soon as you feel up to it, Mrs. Duncan."

It was Christmas Day before Ma felt up to it and then maybe only because Dr. Isaac promised to go with us and come to our house for the rest of the day, if someone didn't take sick and need him.

I was surprised to see Johanna in church with her father and the two little girls. Mrs. Haskell must have stayed home alone. The church was pleasantly warm after the ride in the cold air. I settled into our pew and was looking forward to hearing again the age-old story of the birth of the Christ child. But before the service even began, Reverend Paully introduced a Mr. William Snell who had moved here from Maryland. The man was large, but not fat. He had thinning blond hair and a ruddy face. He sat with Nancy Glover and her family, who Reverend Paully said was Mr. Snell's daughter. Their pew was just across from ours and at first I paid the man little attention. But sometime during the sermon, I noticed him glance our way several times, and it seemed to me he was always looking at Ma. A cold kind of fear knotted my stomach.

When church was over, Johanna and I met in the churchyard for the few minutes we would have before our families were ready to go. From where I stood with Johanna, I could see when Mr. Snell came out of the church. He shook hands with Reverend Paully before turning to gaze about the churchyard. In that moment, I knew who he was searching for and the shock of it made me gasp.

"What's the matter, Annie?" Johanna peered at me, concern in her blue eyes.

"See that man? That Mr. Snell?" I said. "Do you think he has a wife?"

Johanna chuckled. "Well, I'd of thought he'd have brought her to church if he did. Unless," she added, "she's bedfast or something."

"Maybe she is," I said grabbing on to that hope. "Maybe he has someone stay with her at the Glover's."

"He could have a slave woman taking care of her," Johanna said.

I nodded, still clinging to that hope, but knowing, at the same time that if he did have a wife, bedfast or not, Reverend Paully would have said something about her.

Johanna's pa, ready to go, called to her, so we quickly wished each other a happy Christmas. I was anxious to get over to our wagon where Patrick was helping Ma up on the seat. I saw Mr. Snell was making a beeline toward them and I walked as fast as I could, wanting to run, but knowing Ma would have frowned on that and later give me a lecture about how young ladies did not run in public and especially not in the churchyard.

I came up beside the wagon, where Mr. Snell was looking up at Ma with eyes, I now saw, that were pale blue and sort of bulging, like a frog's.

"I lost my dear wife a year ago," he said, speaking just to Ma. *Like the rest of us didn't matter.* "She loved the place, but it was just too lonesome for me. So I sold it lock, stock, and barrel—slaves and all. I plan to buy something here, but I'll take my time in looking."

He talked on; his voice, I noticed, was a little high-pitched, not deep and smooth like Pa's. I might as well have been a stick for all he took notice of me. I didn't think he could see Patrick, either. His eyes, his words, were all just for Ma. A mix of fear and disgust rose up in me. *Was this man thinking of setting his cap for our ma? Was he planning to take Pa's place?* I wanted to scream at him to leave her alone, and my right foot itched to swing forward and kick him. I wished I could chase him across the churchyard and send him back to Maryland, or, at least, to the Glover's farm. Except then, we'd see him again.

Finally, reluctantly, I thought, he tore his eyes from Ma, and seeing Patrick and me, probably for the first time, nodded at us before walking over to his horse.

I got up in the wagon on the seat beside Ma, as Jackson already sat on the front seat with Patrick, where he often held the leather lines "driving" the big black team. I watched as Mr. Snell, or Bug-Eyes as I'd begun to call him in my mind, swing up on his horse. I wished the ground would just open up and swallow him, horse and all. The horse was a beautiful creature that pranced more than walked, its neck arched under a flow of long black mane. The man rode easy, well aware, I was sure, that people were watching him and his beautiful, black, prancing horse.

"Show off," I muttered.

Ma turned toward me. "What?" she said.

"Nothing," I said, not looking at her.

At home we changed into our everyday clothes and sat down to a meal of bread and butter and our favorite soup—a thick, rich, creamy blend of potatoes, carrots, and onions. Ma had baked apple pies for dessert and Dr. Isaac and Patrick each ate two pieces.

Afterwards, Dr. Isaac brought out the gifts he'd brought for us. Patrick was delighted with his new pen and bottle of ink. Jackson made room in an already stuffed stomach for some of his gift, a bag of sweet candies. I took my wide, black velvet ribbon and used the looking glass in Ma's room to tie back my reddish-brown curls. I took so long, admiring how I looked, that Ma called to me to come back and be sociable. She looked pleased with her new handkerchief, edged with lace and with tiny blue flowers embroidered in each corner.

She apologized for not having a gift for Dr. Isaac. She had not bought any of us gifts this year, having not thought of them, she said. Giving Ma a hug, Dr. Isaac drew back and holding her face gently between his two hands, said, "Your company and your children's company, as well as your good cooking, my dear, are all the presents I ever want."

Ma did not mention that Patrick, realizing she would not be getting even Jackson anything this year, had conspired with me to cut back on the things Ma sent us to buy at Mr. McDaniels's store. With what we had saved, we were able to buy our brother a small wood carved wagon with a team of black-painted horses.

Dr. Isaac had also brought us a stack of newspapers he'd saved for Patrick, and that afternoon we sat around reading the news aloud. Some, now, was old news, but interesting just the same. One of the papers had devoted a large column to the new law passed this last September. Called the Compromise of 1850, Dr. Isaac said Congress had passed the law to appease both slave-holding and free states. One major part of the new law was the Fugitive Slave Act that moved the safe boundaries for escaping slaves from the northern, non-slave states to Canada.

Among the news Patrick read aloud to us was an article written by someone opposed to the freeing of slaves. The writer praised the Fugitive Slave Act, saying those in the Underground Railroad, a network of people helping runaway slaves escape into Canada, ought to be taken out and hanged. Fines and jail time would not stop those fool abolitionists, according to the writer, but a few hangings, he was sure, would soon take care of the problem.

We discussed the dangers that the fugitive slaves and the people who aided them risked, and how President Fillmore, who was not a slave owner himself, might feel about the Compromise. We talked about California joining the union as a free state, and how four territories out west—New Mexico, Arizona, Utah, and Nevada—would be allowed to choose to be slave-holding or free when they became states. Patrick thought they would all choose to be free states because he didn't think slavery would be as profitable in those western states. Dr. Isaac wasn't so sure.

Before Dr. Isaac left for home, Ma made us all warm cocoa and set out a plate of raisin cookies. Raisin cookies had always been Pa's favorite. A long ago memory of Pa stealing cookies off the counter where Ma had set them to cool stirred an ache in my heart. In mock anger, Ma had chased him out of the house, flapping her apron at him. I had followed them, standing in the doorway watching, as Pa caught Ma in his arms and gave her a kiss before twirling her around in a little dance. Then with a bow toward her, he had turned away, and whistling a gay tune, had walked with a light, jaunty step to the barn.

"Silly, man," Ma'd said, turning to see me watching from the doorway. But she was smiling.

Chapter Five

Miss McKinley's Party

The first week in January, our teacher, Miss McKinley, announced that she was to be married in a few weeks and would no longer be teaching us. We were all just stunned, for we had no idea she even had a beau. We all liked Miss McKinley, even Ben Gilly, who was not a very good scholar and had a hard time getting his assignments done. She had begun teaching our one-room school six years ago when Patrick was still in school. She was a good teacher, fair to all. Besides, she laughed a lot and hardly anything ever upset her.

At first I wondered who would be taking Miss McKinley's place, and then with a little jump of my heart, I realized there might not be anyone to take her place, and then there would be no school. If the school closed, we would miss all the lessons we had not yet learned, and what if it stayed closed so long that I grew too old for school? Glancing over at Johanna, I saw in her face those same thoughts and fears. We both loved school, but others, like Ben Gilly, would be happy not to have to go anymore. Anxious to know if we would still have school, I raised my hand and asked the question for all of us. "Miss McKinley," I said. "Will we be getting a new teacher?"

A big smile came over her face as she told us a Mr. Ezra Crane, who had come from Pittsburgh, was to fill the position. "He's quite well educated," she said, sounding as pleased as if she had picked him out herself. "They say he's had nearly two years of college."

On the way home that day, Johanna and I had talked about the new teacher. "I hope he's not an old crab," I said.

Johanna laughed. "Me too. But I don't care if he is, I'm just glad to be back in school."

While her ma was sick, Johanna had missed nearly a month of school. But her ma was fine now. She had suffered a bad case of something called morning sickness, which, Johanna explained to me, meant she was going to have a new baby. The baby was to be born sometime in the summer. Johanna wanted it to be a boy, because they didn't have any boys and she knew her pa would especially like a son to work with him on the farm, some day.

On the second day of February, two weeks after Miss McKinley's marriage, a supper was held at the school in her honor. The new teacher, Mr. Ezra Crane, had given us all poems to memorize and recite for the evening's entertainment. The poem he assigned me was called "A Red, Red Rose" by Robert Burns. It was a kind of a love poem and it made me a little bit embarrassed to recite it. But I was saying it perfectly and was almost all the way through it and was feeling quite proud of myself, when I happened to glance over at Mr. Snell. His big, bugged-out eyes were watching Ma, and right then and there, I forgot the poem's last line and Mr. Crane had to prompt me. Oh, but I was mad! *Old Bug-Eyes had no business coming to the party. His children were grown up and his grandchildren were still too little to go to school.* I hated him for making me forget that last line, but more than that, I hated him for looking at Ma, for I knew he was just biding his time until he could come courting.

Johanna ended that part of the program with a Robert Browning poem. She did wonderfully well and I could tell by her smile and the pleased look on her face that she was proud of herself.

Following the program, Miss McKinley, now Mrs. Redkins, was presented a lamp table cover with fringed edges. Johanna's pa was the spokesman for the group and he thanked her on behalf of all the other parents for the many years she had taught their children.

Afterwards the women brought out their supper baskets. The children sat on the floor to eat and the women and young girls used the school benches. The men stood around the outer edges of the room, some leaning against the walls, and balanced their plates in their hands. Mr. Snell stood with is son-in-law, where, of course, he could look at Ma. *Oh, but he made me so mad!*

"What's the matter, Annie?" Johanna whispered. "You're scowling something awful."

I shook my head. "Not now," I whispered through clenched teeth. "I'll tell you later."

But I didn't get a chance to tell Johanna later, for Jackson, who had seemed a little listless now that I thought of it, threw up all over himself and Patrick had to take us home. The next morning Jackson had a high fever and Ma sent Patrick for Dr. Isaac.

Chapter Six

Jackson

Dr. Isaac stayed the night. I slept restlessly, hearing him and Ma move about through the long night hours. In the morning, Jackson was no better and Dr. Isaac stayed with us that day, too. On the morning of the third day, a boy, riding bareback on an old sway-backed white horse, came to ask Dr. Isaac to come see to his mother who, he said, "was terrible sick."

Dr. Isaac kissed Ma's cheek and promised to come back just as soon as he could. "Keep him warm and feed him all the broth he will take," he said, a gentle hand on Ma's arm. "We'll do what we can, Mary, but ultimately he is in God's hands."

While Ma walked Dr. Isaac outside, I sat with Jackson. Ma had a chair pulled up close beside Jackson's bed and I sat on it, watching my little brother for any sign that he needed me. My heart seemed to squeeze inside my chest with every one of his whimpering cries, and I could hardly stand to see his small chest beneath his nightshirt, flutter with each ragged, rasping breath. His shock of red hair on the pillow casing still flamed as red as fire, but his once rosy cheeks had paled to a near white.

I wanted to close my ears to the sound of his whimpers and harsh, raw-sounding coughs and shut my eyes to the sight of his pale face and jerking, fluttering breaths. I did try for a while, squeezing my eyes tight and stopping my ears with my fingers. But I worried then that he would stop breathing and I wouldn't know it. And when Ma came back, he'd be gone. By the time Ma came to relieve me, I had worked myself up into such a state that my ears were buzzing and a dizziness swirled about in my head. I gripped the railing to keep from falling as I went down the steps of the loft, and blindly, I stumbled across the kitchen floor, fumbling for the doorknob. If I didn't soon get to air, I knew I would faint.

The cold air took away the dizziness, but the fear stayed with me—the fear that my little brother was dying. My mind swept me back to Dr. Isaac's little office and the lifeless little babies Ma had rocked and rocked, holding them tight against her chest as her tears fell like the pouring down rain.

Dr. Isaac came back the next evening. His blue eyes looked faded and tired. The white stubble of beard on his usually smooth-shaven chin made him look years older. He had not been able to save the life of the boy's mother and sorrow was in every line of his face. It was hard for him when a patient died. I knew it would nearly kill him if we lost Jackson.

Fear and loneliness followed me through the long, long days and visited my dreams at night. Each morning, I woke with the memory of those haunting, frightening dreams, sometimes so vivid I would think for a moment they were real. The dreams and the constant work throughout the day left me always tired. I seemed to be always cooking or washing dishes, or scrubbing clothes or floors… and I missed school so much. Mr. Ezra Crane was squatty in stature and a bit sour-faced, just the opposite of Miss McKinley's slender, tall frame and sunny smile, but I liked him all right. He'd brought a new supply of books with him and often read aloud to us and I had so enjoyed that. I missed Johanna, too. I knew now how Johanna had felt having to stay home when her mother was ill.

One evening, I pushed supper to the back of the stove to keep warm until Patrick had the chores finished. The need to be out and away from the sounds of Jackson's harsh, labored breathing and ragged coughs sent me outside into the gathering darkness and down the path to the barn.

My shadow, cast in the lantern's light, leaped across the walls as I pushed open the door. Patrick, stooping to pick up the milk stool, straightened abruptly, the stool slipping from his hand. "Annie!" he said sharply.

"Sorry," I said and turned over an empty feed bucket to sit on. The barn was warm and the familiar musky scent of the animals, hay, and manure was somehow comforting. Elbows on my knees, my chin cupped between my hands, I watched Patrick's hands move in a steady rhythm as he milked Blossom, and my thoughts went back to that day last fall when Johanna and I had run into the old man bringing back our cow. "Un'spected guests," he had said, and he had "borryed" Blossom's milk to feed them. There had been a young'un, he'd said. I wondered again about the child and the age it might have been.

Wrapped in my thoughts, hardly even aware of the sound of milk squirting steadily into the bucket under Blossom's udder,

I jumped when Patrick, his head still against Blossom's flank, his hands still keeping the steady squeeze and pull on Blossom's teats, said, "I've been thinking, Annie, wondering if we should stay here on this farm."

His words shocked me. What would we do? Go to Burns Ferry… To Pittsburgh… *Did Patrick still have it in his head to study law?*

As if in answer to my thoughts, Patrick said, "I won't be able to study law. I don't care much for farming and I'll have to make a living for us. Unless… If Ma remarries…"

Old Bug-Eyes popped into my head and a shiver ran down my spine. Would he come one day courting Ma? Would she accept his courting? Would she marry him? A sickness washed over me and my stomach lurched, bringing up a sour taste. "Maybe we could move," I said to Patrick. "Maybe that would be the best." Under my breath I added, "And let's go before Old Bug-Eyes comes courting, if he's bound to."

Chapter Seven

Spinner

I sat at the table staring at the mess of breakfast dishes to be washed and put away. Last night I dreamed that Jackson had died and the dream's images played over and over in my head—images of Ma and Patrick beside Jackson's bed, sobbing. In my dream, I said, "He's not dead. Look at him!" In disbelief, I leaned over him to catch a whisper of breath from his parted lips, but none came. I stumbled back and tears burst from my eyes. Suddenly, Towser leaped up on the bed and began to lick Jackson's still, white face. Immediately color bloomed on Jackson's cheeks and he sat up, laughing, and wrapped his little arms about the old black dog.

Dreams do not mean a thing, I told myself. If they did, Pa would be home. Still I couldn't keep the images of the dream out of my head and all morning they kept me constantly swallowing tears. I was doing the dishes from our midday meal when I thought of how Jackson, when sad or upset, had taken comfort from Towser, his arms around the old dog's neck, his face buried in his black coat, and with that thought came another hitting me like a sudden strike of lightning. *The Haskell dog! That small tan-colored one! Maybe I could get that dog for Jackson!*

With hope running high, I hurried through my work. I meant to ask Ma about the dog, but when the time came to go, I just said, "Johanna will be getting out of school soon. Would it be all right if I ran to meet her?" Ma, holding Jackson and spoon-feeding him tiny sips of broth, frowned, and quickly I jumped in with, "I won't be long, and I'll come right back to start supper."

Ma's face softened and I knew she would let me go. She shifted Jackson to a more comfortable position in her arms, and with a little nod of her head said, "All right. I expect you do miss Johanna."

"I do," I acknowledged and started to turn away when Ma put her hand on my arm.

"You have helped me so much, Annie. I don't know what I'd do without you."

I felt my face flush as the warmth of her words settled in my heart. "I'm glad I can help you, Ma," I said and swallowed the quick rise of tears.

The winter sun hung low in the sky, offering little warmth. I pulled my muffler up over my nose as I hurried to meet Johanna. Although I had hardly been able to wait to ask about the dog, when Johanna, smiling and waving, hurried toward me, I grew suddenly afraid. *What if the dog was gone? What if they wanted to keep him?*

We exchanged greetings and I asked about her family, and she, in turn, asked about mine. Then I blurted out, "Do you still have that dog? That stray?"

"Yes," she said, a puzzled frown wrinkling her brow. "Why do you ask?"

"Could I have him? For Jackson? A d—dog might help him get b—better," I managed before tears clogged my throat.

"Oh, my goodness. Of course, Annie. Let's go get him right away." Johanna pulled a handkerchief from her pocket and offering it to me with a soft smile, said, "Here, wipe those tears before they freeze on your face."

As we came in sight of Johanna's home, the dogs ran out to greet us, the small tan one among them. He wiggled up to me, so eagerly affectionate, that I couldn't help but laugh. "Jackson's going to just love you," I said.

Ma suggested we name him Spinner as he had a habit of spinning around and around in pursuit of his tail, a puppy trait he had never outgrown. "Although, goodness knows," Ma said, "he is hardly more than that now."

Jackson seemed to rally almost as soon as the dog leaped up on his bed and licked his face. But although Spinner was to be Jackson's dog, it was clear that he favored Patrick. One evening, watching from the window as the two roughhoused their way to the barn, I commented on how much the dog liked Patrick.

"Hush," Ma said. "Jackson will hear you."

Chapter Eight

Sugar Weather

Jackson grew stronger as February gave way to March and the sweet sap in the maple trees began to run. With the sap running, it was time to go out among the trees and gather the clear liquid to boil over open fires until it had turned to syrup, maple cream, or the sweet delicious maple sugar candy.

Mr. William Snell had begun courting Ma now that Jackson was recovering, and he insisted on helping us with our sugaring off. He said his daughter's family had plenty of help, so he'd be free to give us a hand. He said it like it was a blessing of sorts, like we couldn't help but be overjoyed with his daily presence. I nearly threw up.

Ma smiled. It looked to me like a sick, little smile, but her voice was gay and charming. "Why Mr. Snell," she said, "how kind of you."

"I insist you call me William," he said, grandly, as if, I thought, clenching my teeth, *He is stooping to mix with us common folks.*

He was the one who decided that Jackson should not go out

in the sugar bush, as he might get a setback and this time might not recover. He didn't say it exactly like that, but it scared Ma. I saw the look on her face. Suddenly, fresh air and sunshine gave way to housebound and plenty of blankets, just in case. The sly devil had planned on me staying in with Jackson, leaving Ma free to be with him. But worry nixed those plans and Ma stayed with Jackson, leaving *lucky me* with the pleasure of working with Bug-Eyes.

Our stand of sugar maples produced well, the sap dripping steadily into the buckets we'd hung from the trees. The weather cooperated, too, but I hated every day of it.

It was hard work, but I had always enjoyed it until this year with Old Bug-Eyes helping us. When I groused about it to Patrick, he said, "You knew it wouldn't be the same anyway, Annie. Not without Pa."

Pa hadn't been here to help us last year either, but I didn't point that out to Patrick—I knew what he meant. Last year, we still had a pa, even if he was riding across some wilderness to get to California, instead of here helping us with the sugaring off.

Those days in the sugar bush, I sure saw the bossy side of Bug-Eyes. You would have thought he, and not Ma, owned this particular stand of maple trees. He knew *everything*! The best way to tap the trees… How much wood to have on hand… Patrick had cut a stack of wood for our sugar fires, but it wasn't, according to him, quite enough, so he ordered some more from a woodcutter. After sugaring off was over, we had a whole stack of wood left, but no one mentioned it. Old Bug-Eyes even criticized the scouring of the buckets we used to gather the sap. At first I thought he'd make us scour them over again, but he didn't. He drove Nick and Ned from tree to tree and back to the fire with the buckets of sap, but Patrick and I loaded the buckets while he waited scowling and impatient looking, like he thought we weren't hurrying fast enough.

Of course, he was all just honey-pie and helpful when Ma, leaving Jackson with Spinner in the house for company, came out to bring our midday meals and to check on our progress.

Those days in the sugar bush were beautiful weather days. The sun a golden glow of warmth by day, the nights still brisk and cold. "Good sugar weather," Dr. Isaac said, the days he could join us.

I had always loved the smell of the clear liquid boiling into golden syrup in the iron kettles set over the fires. But the sweet, flower like scent, mingled with the heavier, darker odor of the wood fires gave me no pleasure this year. This year I just wanted it to be over so we wouldn't have to see Old Bug-Eyes every single day. But even when the trees began to bud out, the sap now too strong for sugar or syrup, and we left the sugar bush until next year, we still saw way too much of him to suit me. Although, not to see him at all would suit me the best. I was always thankful for those days when, for some reason or other, he didn't come to see Ma, but he didn't miss many days.

He must have thought that we all sat idle each afternoon with nothing to do but to entertain him, for that's when he usually showed up. I suppose in his old life, slaves did most of the work, so the white folks could while away every afternoon, sipping drinks and nibbling on sweets. I wished Ma would tell him that we had to work extra hard to make up for the hours we spent with him. Or better still, tell him to leave and not come back. But, of course, she didn't do either. I suppose she was lonely and enjoyed his company, but she never laughed or teased in his presence as she used to do with Pa.

I often thought of my dream of riding behind Pa on Big Jake. It had been so real I could almost imagine that one day my dream would come true. I knew it was foolish, but I couldn't help it. I knew Pa was gone. He would never be back. Dreams did not foretell the future. I had dreamed of Jackson's death and he had lived. I had dreamed of a live Towser and he was already dead. Dreams were dreams and that was all. Just stories your head made up out of your worries and hopes while you slept.

After the letter, Ma had stopped talking about Pa. I had tried, and so had Patrick, to get her to talk with us about our memories of him. "Remember the time when Pa," one of us would begin, and Ma would get up and go to her room. We would stare after her and neither Patrick nor I ever continued whatever it was we had started to say. Sometimes now Ma would say something about Pa, but always it was about the farm, like she might say to Patrick, "You had best get that fence fixed before the cows get out. Your pa would have done it right away."

As Patrick said, "Well, even getting bawled out about not being as good as Pa is better than not hearing about him at all."

"I suppose," I'd said to him that day, "you won't even hear that if Ma marries Old Bug-Eyes. I don't think he's going to let her even mention Pa's name. Leastways, I don't think so. I think he's too selfish to share anything that doesn't include him."

One night in my bed, thinking such thoughts, the round white moon shining in through my window, casting a splash of pale light across my room, I thought of how sometimes my parents had yelled at each other. Once they had argued over this window. Ma said it was too large and too expensive and not at all necessary. But Pa had insisted I needed the window.

"Without the window, it's nothing more than a chicken coop," he had said of the little room. "Do you want your daughter in a chicken coop?" Ma had laughed then and he'd laughed, too. They quarreled, all right. But they laughed more. If Ma married Old Bug-Eyes, I was certain there would be no arguments, for only his way would be right. And as for laughter... well, so far I hadn't seen a speck of humor in the man.

Chapter Nine

A Nest of Copperheads

The moon came out of the gathering clouds and shone down on the prone body of the red wolf. In death, the fierce jaws had released the old speckled hen, but it, too, was dead. Aroused from sleep by Spinner barking, we had tumbled out of bed, Patrick grabbing the gun as he went out the door. He shot the animal as it came out of the chicken house, the hen limp in its mouth.

As Patrick knelt to examine the carcass, he noted aloud that the wolf had pups she hadn't yet weaned, and that one of her back legs had been broken. "I'm afraid the old girl was desperate," he said. "Crippled like she was, she must have had a tough time catching anything to eat. I expect that's why she risked coming here."

Ma frowned. "She looks to be just skin stretched over bone."

"I know." Patrick sighed. "I bet her mate's dead, too. In a way I wish my shot would have missed her."

"Except she'd have been back," Ma said. "I'm not overly fond of feeding all of our hens to a wolf family." She lifted her gaze to the dark, jagged outline of the mountains, muttered something, and went back to the house.

I had trouble sleeping the rest of the night. I kept imagining the baby wolves huddled in their den, whimpering for their mother. They must have been on Patrick's mind, too, for the next day, when it started raining early in the morning, making the fields too muddy to work, he took Spinner and his gun and headed up into the hills.

The rain stopped by midmorning and the sun came out hot and bright. By noontime or soon after, we expected to see Patrick come down out of the hills, Spinner at his side. But by chore time, he still wasn't home.

"Well, let's get the milking done," Ma said. "I can't imagine what's keeping him."

We milked all the cows but Blossom. We had let her go dry as she was due to have a new calf later this spring. Ma split up enough wood to fill the wood box, and I fed the chickens and the hogs.

At bedtime, Ma took Jackson up into the loft and put him to bed. Afterwards she started a small fire in the stove. "I'll heat some water for tea," she said.

It had been hot and steamy after the rain, but with sundown, a north wind had risen, chilling the air. The tea, though warm and soothing, did not take away the cold fear that was growing in me—the fear that something had happened to Patrick.

We sat side by side, Ma in her big rocker, her feet on the little stool Pa had made for her one Christmas. I sat in Pa's chair, my feet curled up under me. We said little to each other, our ears tuned to catch any sound that would mean Patrick was home. But only the wind in the trees and the occasional call of an owl disturbed the silence of the night.

I wished Pa could be here, if only for just this little while. He would have gone hours ago to look for Patrick, "reading sign," as he'd have called the hunt for whatever faint trail Patrick and Spinner had left behind. Pa's keen eyes saw what most of us could not. From partial footprints, to bent grass and broken twigs, he read the woods as easily as Patrick read words in a book. I was dwelling on those thoughts, my mind's eye seeing Pa moving silently through the trees with careful steps, open ears, and searching eyes, when Ma said, "Maybe I was a fool for letting your pa go off to California without us."

Startled, I uncurled my feet and dropped them to the floor. "What?" I said.

Sadness filled Ma's eyes. "I know there's no place where we'll always be safe," she said. "No way we can tell what's coming, good or bad."

"Is that why we didn't go with Pa?" I asked. "Because you thought something would happen to us?"

"Yes, Annie. When we moved here from our farm in New York, the twins took sick on the way… It was cold and rainy…" She pulled a handkerchief from her apron pocket and wiped her eyes and nose. "When they died, I vowed I'd never move again. Never risk the lives of my children, ever again."

"But we are all older than the twins were, even Jackson. And I bet Dr. Isaac would have gone with us."

"No," Ma said. "He thought he was too old. But even if he had agreed to go with us…Well, even he can't cure everything."

"Didn't Pa worry about us getting sick?"

"Oh, yes. He was heartsick when the twins died, but he said they might have taken sick anyway. That life will always be uncertain and we can't hide from it. He was right, although I do think it is safer when we stay in one place. Still, we could have an outbreak of diphtheria or heaven knows what else right here." Again, she wiped her eyes with the handkerchief and shoving it back into her apron pocket, said, "If we'd have gone to California, everything might have turned out fine, or it might not have. There is no way to know what will happen when or where, until it does."

I nodded, not knowing what to say.

Ma got up out of her chair and picked up a small chunk of wood from the wood box to add to the fire. Frowning, she turned back to me, the wood still in her hand.

"Jackson's last bout of illness was terribly serious. For a time I thought we'd lose him. I…" Her voice trailed off and she turned back to the stove and opening the stove lid, shoved the chunk of wood inside, jiggling it with the poker down into the coals. When the fire flamed up, she replaced the lid and turned back to me. "Mr. Snell told me his wife died from the measles. We usually get the measles when we're children. Grownups can have a terribly hard time with them."

I noticed Ma still called Bug-Eyes Mr. Snell, except to his face.

"Mrs. Snell had lived all her life on her family's farm," Ma continued. "Her father being dead, Mr. Snell took over the farm after they married." She shrugged. " Maybe she wouldn't have taken sick if they'd have moved somewhere else."

Sudden anger stirred in me. Unreasonable, I knew, but I could not stop it. Why didn't Ma tell Bug-Eyes to go find someone else to be his wife? And why had Pa left us? He knew there was danger in such a long journey. Didn't he know that he might not come back? Gold couldn't have been that important to him. But maybe his wanderlust was. Maybe even more important than his family. And Patrick… Why did he have to go off and look for those wolf pups? He was going to kill them anyway. Put them out of their misery—keep them from starving to death. Now he was hurt, or lost, or something… A cold, sick feeling washed over me and tears welled up, hot and stinging.

"Annie," Ma took a step toward me. "What—"

A sudden commotion at the door interrupted her and drove away my tears as it sent my heart to racing. We stared, motionless, as the door opened, and to our relief we saw Patrick standing in the doorway.

Ma would say later that Patrick looked like he'd been in a fight with a wild cat. Scratched and dirty, he hopped into the room on one foot, steadying himself with a stout stick. A torn piece of his shirt bound his ankle and his face looked stricken and pale as death.

"Patrick!" Ma ran to him and took his arm. "My dear! What happened!"

"I'm all right, Ma." Patrick groaned out the words. "But Spinner's dead, and I think my ankle's broken."

Hot tea and a blanket warmed Patrick enough so he could tell us about Spinner without his teeth chattering. "I was searching for those wolf pups... climbing over some rocks, and like a fool didn't watch where I was going. I stepped in a nest of copperheads. They gave warning... buzzed at me. I jumped backwards. Fell... My foot caught in a crevice of rock. That's when I hurt my ankle. I was out of danger, but I guess Spinner didn't realize it." Patrick looked down at the cup of tea in his hands. The hurt on his face brought quick tears to my eyes.

When he could speak again, he said, "I kept yelling, but he just wouldn't quit. He was going to kill every last one of them. I guess he thought they had hurt me. They bit him a number of times."

"He was a small dog," Ma said. "It wouldn't take much to poison him."

"I stayed with him until he died." Patrick's voice faltered, then steadied. "He didn't suffer long."

I leaned toward him. "Where's your gun?" I asked.

He jerked his head toward the door. "I used it and this stick as crutches to get home. I left it outside, leaning by the door."

"Did you find the wolf pups?"

He shook his head.

Ma drove Patrick into Burns Ferry to see Dr. Isaac. I stayed with Jackson, who slept through it all. They were back home at daybreak. After breakfast, Ma and I went up into the hills to get Spinner. As we walked back, Ma carrying Spinner's body wrapped in the old piece of ragged quilt she'd brought along, I thought about the old she-wolf and her pups. Because she had been old and crippled, she had raided our henhouse and now she was dead, and probably her babies, too. And because of them, Patrick had a broken ankle and Spinner was dead. It seemed to me that when you least expect it, something happens that causes something else to happen, and our lives are changed. One day we're going along, not expecting trouble, and then a wolf comes calling.

Chapter Ten

William's Sunday Visit

I stood at the door looking out at the beautiful green hills surrounding our farm. A whisper of a breeze stirred the leaves in the oak tree beside the front door; and from somewhere among its branches came the sweet, lilting notes of a little brown wren. It was a beautiful day, but one I would just as soon have skipped over. It was another Sunday and another whole day with Bug-Eyes. I shifted my gaze toward the barn lot where the new hired man was harnessing Nick and Ned so we could go to church. Bug-Eyes and Patrick stood watching, Patrick leaning on his crutches, a scowl, I was certain, on his face. Patrick hated not being able to do the work and was not at all pleased with the shifty-eyed man Bug-Eyes had taken upon himself to hire for us. He had wanted to buy us a slave. But Ma's old fiery temper came back, as fierce as it used to be before we knew Pa wasn't coming home. *Before her heart broke.* I surprised myself with this sudden knowledge of my mother and felt a stab of pain at the memory of her grief in those awful days after the letter. I knew I would always wonder if Mrs. Haskell hadn't forced her to get out of bed, if we'd even have our ma with us now, or would she be in the tiny cemetery beside the twins? I wished Pa could be there with those babies, not buried in some lonely grave where no one knew or cared about him. An awful thought followed that one and before I could dash it out of my mind; it grew and attached itself to me so vividly I could not shake it off. What if Pa lay uncovered somewhere, his body ripped by wolves and buzzards until only his bones lay scattered across that wild land?

To keep the tears from spilling over, I made myself recall how Ma, when Bug-Eyes said he would buy her a slave, had turned on him, eyes flashing with their old fire. "I am not having a slave," she told him. "If you know of a freed man who needs work, I'll consider him. But, I will have no slaves."

Bug-Eyes has a cold kind of a smile, sometimes. His irritated smile, I call it. He smiled that smile at Ma then, and in a voice turned smooth as honey but hard as nails, too, said the decision was hers for now. But after they were married, he'd decide how best to run the farm.

Ma didn't say anything to that, but her face got red, and after he left she sort of slammed things around in the kitchen, muttering under her breath. Her anger gave me hope, and I thought it was too bad Bug-Eyes had gone back outside and didn't see the slamming part. I thought if he could see how angry she could get, he might rethink his marriage proposal. It bothered me, too, that Ma wanted to marry the man, even though he made her so angry. Of course, Pa had made her angry, too, but he had also made her laugh. And that made all the difference.

It was odd how Bug-Eyes had proposed. Right after Patrick got hurt, he rode over on his beautiful, black horse and without even getting down out of the saddle, asked Ma to marry him. No fanfare… no romantic words… He just sat up on that big, beautiful, black animal, so skittish he has to keep it reined in tight for it to stand even halfway still, and said, "Mary, you're going to be needing help with this farm now that Patrick's laid up. I don't see any use in us putting off getting married now. Do you?"

Ma said if he'd get off that horse and come inside they'd talk about it.

So he did. Patrick and Jackson and I stayed outside.

Ma never did say she was marrying him. She just said, "Mr. Snell will be in charge of the farm the first of September." And in the next breath, she told Patrick he could go ahead with his plan to apprentice out to that lawyer friend of Dr. Isaac's in Pittsburgh.

The first of September. I swung my gaze back to the hills and thought of Pa, of his brown twinkling eyes and wide warm smile and a terrible longing swept over me, bringing tears. I shook my head, banishing the tears, though not the sadness, and turned and stepped back inside to pick up my bonnet for church.

The Reverend Paully's sermon was, as usual, long and drawn out, and my attention often wandered. Once, hearing the word slaves, I sat up straighter and listened, but I had missed too many other words to make any sense of the sermon.

Ma had invited Dr. Isaac to come home with us for Sunday dinner. Bug-Eyes, of course, would come, too. Dr. Isaac accepted Ma's invitation, but Slim Raften, a neighbor of ours, came for him, pulling his light buggy up into the churchyard just as we were all coming out the door. Samuel, his youngest boy, had fallen out of a tree and they feared his leg was broken, so Dr. Isaac left with him, and we were stuck with just Bug-Eyes.

After dinner, Jackson went outside to play. I envied him as

I went to sit with Patrick and Ma to entertain Bug-Eyes. At first, we talked about the church. I asked what Reverend Paully had said about slaves. "Surely, as a man of God, he doesn't believe in slavery." I directed my words to Bug-Eyes out of spite and stressing the word *God.* I wanted him to know that I thought even God didn't like slavery.

Bug-Eyes laughed. "The good Reverend was speaking strictly of Biblical times."

"Also that the master should treat the slave with kindness," Ma said.

Bug-Eyes snorted like a horse. "You can't be too good to your coloreds," he said. "They're born connivers, and lazy to boot. They'd sooner lie and steal than work. Those fool abolitionist folks don't know what they're doing, setting them free. Why they'd be like a plague amongst us. Like the locusts and flies in Moses' time, swarming everywhere." A frown drew his pale eyebrows over his bugged-out eyes, and he added as if an afterthought, "Besides, it's like turning loose someone's livestock."

"I could not liken them to animals," Ma said. "They are, I'm sure, quite human."

Bug-Eyes turned his gaze on Ma. "Maybe a low form of human. That's why they're property with folks paying as much as a thousand dollars for a good, strong one."

"Slave holding is a part of the trouble among us Virginians," Patrick said. "I'm sure you know about the Convention in Richmond."

Bug-Eyes nodded. "There's even talk in those sessions of these western counties forming a new state, independent of the east, and calling it West Virginia. It's a bunch of nonsense, I say."

"I wish women could vote," Ma said.

Bug-Eyes laughed long and loud at that. "Women voting?" he sneered. "Why the coloreds will be voting sooner than women." He laughed again. "And that means never."

Abruptly Ma stood up, two bright spots of color on her cheeks. "I'd better see what Jackson's doing," she said.

I couldn't help but grin. Ma wasn't worried about Jackson. He played outside all the time. She was just giving herself time to cool off. *Keep it up, Bug-Eyes,* I thought, gleefully, *and Ma's liable to send you packin'.*

Dismissing Ma with a casual glance, Bug-Eyes turned to Patrick. "I gather you think slavery ought to be abolished. And I gather, too, that if one of those runaways came by here, you'd give him sanction. Even though," he added stressing the words, "it's against the law."

"The law is wrong," Patrick said.

"But it is the law." Old Bug-Eyes looked smug as a cat licking cream off its whiskers. "You want to be a lawyer. Are you going to be a lawyer who breaks the law?"

Patrick frowned. "I don't know. But I'm not a lawyer, yet."

I could see anger building in Patrick, flushing his cheeks and darkening his blue eyes, and I was glad when Ma came back inside and the talk turned to other things.

Bug-Eyes had heard that Mr. McDaniels had put his store and post office up for sale, and they talked about that for a while.

"I expect his rheumatism is getting the best of him," Ma said. "It's too bad for he's not that old of a man."

After Mr. McDaniels and his store, the weather was discussed, and, finally, thankfully for me and I knew for Patrick as well, the afternoon passed and Bug-Eyes brought his visit to an end.

Later that evening Blossom gave birth to a little red calf, a miniature of herself. "So the day wasn't a total loss," Patrick whispered aside to me.

Chapter Eleven

The Runaway

As much as I dreaded Sundays and the afternoons that Bug-Eyes came to call, I dreaded more the approaching marriage. What would I do when he and Ma were married and he lived with us every day? How could I stand it to have that man in our house... I corrected myself... in his house, for it would be his then. Even my little room, I was sure, he'd consider his. I wished I were old enough to live on my own. Maybe I could teach school, or be a midwife, or, as long as I was dreaming, buy Mr. McDaniels's store. That was really what I would rather do. I knew I would enjoy waiting on people, all the while visiting with them as Mr. McDaniels always did. I would have liked to have gone to Burns Ferry today just to visit the store, but I was not going anywhere with Bug-Eyes if I didn't *have* to go.

He had come by early this morning with his son-in-law's wagon to pick up Ma and Jackson. He wanted to build an addition on to the house after he and Ma were married and was anxious to have the lumber stacked and ready. With his soft hands, I was quite sure he wouldn't do any of the building himself, but would, by then, have slave labor. There wasn't going to be any way Ma could stop him either—not then, not when he was her husband. Bug-Eyes always had to be telling folks what to do. No wonder he liked slavery so much. It scared me to think that Ma, after she married him, might be as much a slave to him as the real ones would be. Even her anger would not free her then. I was afraid that if Ma ever went against his wishes, once they were married and she was his wife, his possession, his property, that she would probably get a tongue lashing. But what scared me the most was that he might also raise a hand to her. Yet Ma never seemed concerned, so maybe I was wrong. I sure hoped so. But it was certain she'd not be having her way once they married, not in managing the farm, anyway, for he had made that clear the day he'd wanted to buy her a slave. I thought he might as well have added to that declaration, "And you will be mine and have no say in the matter." I knew that even though Ma did not believe in slavery, she would soon be the mistress of a slave or two. But she would, I knew, treat them well, if Bug-Eyes would allow her to do so.

Those thoughts roaming around in my head, sometimes causing tears, sometimes angry mutterings under my breath, I spent the morning with the mending basket, sewing up rips, replacing buttons, and patching holes in the knees and elbows of several garments. Patrick had been out fixing fence since daylight. At midday he came in and ate and then went to the barn to oil Nick and Ned's harnesses.

Our noonday meal had left me with a craving for something sweet, so I decided to make a cobbler of strawberries and rhubarb for supper tonight and surprise Ma. I knew the wild strawberries that grew on the sunny slope above the twins' small graveyard were ripe now and when I finished the mending, I took a berry basket and climbed the hill back of the house.

At the little, fenced-in cemetery, I stopped to admire the wild pink roses Ma had planted on the twins' single grave. A bumblebee buzzed among the blossoms and a soft breeze lifted the sweet scent from the roses, perfuming the air. I breathed deeply, thinking I would know the smell of wild roses anywhere, when a sound caught my ear and sent a chill sweeping through me. *Someone was in that stand of red maples.* I froze, my heart leaping in my chest, my mouth suddenly dry as dust. My eyes darted here and there, sweeping across and up and down the hillside and back to the trees where a sudden movement caught my eye. The hair on my neck lifted and I jerked back a step. Eyes fastened on that spot where I'd seen the movement, I saw a man stumble from the trees. Cold shock flooded through me, and a scream ripped from my throat.

At my scream, the man reared back, arms flailing. He turned as if to run back into the maples, but his legs crumpled and he sprawled face forward on the ground.

I stared at the heap of tattered clothing... the dark skin on the bare, outstretched arms... the mat of black hair on the motionless head.... And the knowledge that this was a runaway slave flashed through my head like shooting sparks from the hot coals of a stirred-up fire. I jerked around to look in all directions, certain that at any moment slave catchers would burst into the clearing, guns in hand. I had heard that slave catchers often used dogs to run down escaping slaves, and the thought that dogs might, at any moment, run out of the trees chilled me to the bone. My eyes skipped over the body of the man to again race up and down and across the hillside, but the only movement I detected was the fluttering motion of the leaves on the nearby trees. The only sound to reach my straining ears was the sighing of a little breeze.

I turned again to the man lying still as death, and fearfully took a step forward. I would have to help him. Somehow... I, who was against slavery, could not leave him here, if alive, at the mercy of the slave catchers. Maybe I could get him down the hill to our place. Maybe we could hide him in the barn. I forced myself to take a step toward him, my heart hammering hard enough to break through my chest. Suddenly a squirrel chattered and my resolve vanished. I turned and flew down the hill toward the safety of home.

Patrick heard my running footsteps and came to meet me at the barn door, limping out of the dark shadows into the sunlight. In a rush of words, I told him about the runaway.

"We'd better get him hidden and quick before William gets here," Patrick said.

"William!" I cried. "O mercy. I forgot about William."

Patrick's frown grew dark. "We'll put him in the barn," he said. "You'll have to help me, Annie."

I shivered. "I know," I said. I was glad the hired man had been let go, for he would have been as much of a danger to us, and the runaway, as Bug-Eyes. Patrick's ankle had healed in the two months since the accident and Spinner's death, although it had left him with a slight limp. Never having liked or trusted the man Bug-Eyes had hired to help with the farm work, Patrick had insisted he was now capable of doing the work himself and, reluctantly, Bug-Eyes had let him go.

Patrick brought Ned up from the pasture to carry the man home. He was the calmer of our two big workhorses. Patrick bridled him so the blinders would shield some of his view, but even so the horse tried to pull back, snorting his distrust and fear when he saw the man on the ground.

The man, so thin he was nearly skeletal, was nevertheless dead weight. Patrick grunted, the sweat popping out on his forehead, as he lifted the limp form and pushed him up on Ned.

Ned tried to step away from them, eyes wide and nostrils flaring, but I kept a tight grip on the bridle ring and stroked his neck murmuring over and over, "Easy, Ned. It's all right boy. Easy."

With the man up on the horse, his head and arms dangling down on one side of Ned's bare back, his legs on the other, Patrick came around and took the bridle ring from my hand.

"Walk beside him," Patrick commanded. "So if he starts to slip off, you can grab him."

I nodded; the lump of fear in my throat had grown to a monstrous size. My heart thumped and hammered, and my legs had grown impossibly wobbly and weak.

When, at last, we got him into the barn, laid up against a cushion of hay behind the manger, I ran to the house for water. Patrick splashed a little on the man's face. He came to slowly at first and then with a jerk, his eyes flying open in a look of absolute terror.

"We're friends," Patrick said as the man tried frantically to get to his feet.

"Friends?" the man whispered and sank back, tears coming to his eyes. "I... I... sure does thank..."

"Eat," Patrick interrupted. "You can talk later."

I had stuffed some cold biscuits into my pocket when I went for the water, and Patrick gave them to the man, who wolfed them down and tried again to speak "I be—"

"Quiet!" Patrick hissed. "Listen!"

The terror that had eased some in the shelter of the barn slammed back. "What is it?" I whispered.

"A wagon," Patrick said. "It's got to be Ma and William." He turned back to the runaway. "Stay here," he said grimly, "and don't you make a sound."

While Patrick helped Bug-Eyes unload the lumber, Jackson

sat on the wagon seat, where Bug-Eyes had commanded him to stay so he'd not get in their way. I walked to the house with Ma and told her about the runaway slave.

She listened as calmly as if we hid fugitive slaves in the barn everyday. As we stepped into the house, she turned to me, a big grin splashed across her face. "I believe, my dear," she said, "I'm going to get terribly ill."

I stared at her, for a moment not grasping what she was saying. When I caught on, I giggled. "You startled me, Ma," I said.

The grin lingering, her eyes gleaming with a hint of mischief, Ma told me to run and tell Bug-Eyes she wasn't feeling well and that he should go on home. The grin disappeared with her next words and her eyes grew serious. "As soon as William is gone, we'll send Patrick into town for Dr. Isaac and have him bring back a quarantine sign."

Chapter Twelve

Under Quarantine

"Will they know what contagious means?" I asked, watching Dr. Isaac tack the quarantine sign up on our front door. I was a little anxious about depending on a sign to keep the slave catchers from coming into our house—into my room—to get the runaway.

"Most people have seen this sign," Dr. Isaac assured me, "Even if they can't read, they'll know there's sickness in the house. Even the most foolhardy won't risk that."

Dr. Isaac had insisted we move the man out of the barn and into the house. "He tells me two men picked up his trail some days ago—he wasn't sure how many—a week or two I suspect, and he's been running from them ever since. The frown on his face deepened as he added, "They'll show up here sooner or later and I think it will be safer for you and for him, too, if he's in the house. They'll search the barn right away and it's doubtful he could escape without being seen."

Patrick suggested putting him down in the cellar under the kitchen floor, but Dr. Isaac thought about my room. "In the cellar he'd be like a rat in a trap," he said. "In Annie's room, he'll have a window if he needs to leave in a hurry. It's at the back of the house and just a quick sprint to the trees."

So they decided. *Everyone but me. A colored man in my room? Sleeping in my bed?* It had given me the shivers then and it gave me the shivers now.

His name, he told us, was Henry. He had no last name and would not, he said, take the name of his owner. "When I gets to Canada," he told us, "I be choosin' a name to be mine."

At first, Ma hadn't liked the idea of having Henry in the house and in my room any more than I did. "If he stays in the barn, we can take turns keeping watch," she told Dr. Isaac. "If they show up, we can holler out that we've sickness here. Henry could slip out then, and perhaps we could keep them engaged a while. We might even ask them if they could please ride to Burns Ferry for the doctor. That should make it sound as if we really did have a sickness here." She thought a moment, frowning. Finally shaking her head, she said, "But what if they came in the dark and we'd not see them?"

"You don't even have a dog to warn you," Dr. Isaac said.

"Maybe we could borrow one from the Haskells," I said. My sudden idea pleased me and gave me hope that the man could stay in the barn. "They've got lots of dogs."

"We can't tell anyone about Henry," Dr. Isaac reminded me. "Not even the Haskells."

"Well," I said. "Couldn't we say we've got deer eating the garden?"

A slight frown wrinkled his brow. "That might work. I'll chew on that awhile." He turned to Ma. "But until I get that dog, if I do, we'd still better put Henry in Annie's room."

Patrick, listening to us, said, "I've heard slave catchers often use dogs to track down a runaway. Those two hunting Henry might have dogs."

Dr. Isaac frowned. "Well, so far, they don't. Henry said he had some close calls, but if the men had had dogs, he was sure they would have caught him long ago." He paused and then added, "They could have picked up some by now, though."

I shivered, imagining myself a black slave, running, dogs snapping at my heels.

Anxious to be getting back to Burns Ferry to begin his cautious inquiry about getting our guest on his way through the Underground Railroad, Dr. Isaac would not stay for supper. "The sooner we get this taken care of, the better," he said. "Those men tailing Henry are likely to show up here any time now."

Patrick, who stood at the window, his eyes and ears on constant alert for the men the runaway said had been chasing him, asked, "Do you think there are some Underground folks in Burns Ferry?"

The image of the old man in the woods who had "borryed" Blossom flashed into my mind and I said, "Maybe you could take him to old Mr. Looney Barnes."

Dr. Isaac laughed. "We aren't that desperate yet. Even a runaway ought not to have to put up with Looney's smelly old shack." With a wink at me, he turned back to Patrick.

"To answer your question, son, I'm quite confident I know of someone who, if he isn't engaged in the Underground's work, will know who I can contact."

Patrick frowned. "Be careful," he said.

"I will." A sudden grin chased away Dr. Isaac's somber look. " I've no desire to spend my latter years behind bars."

Dr. Isaac was also anxious to stop at the Glovers to tell Bug-Eyes about Ma's pretend illness so he wouldn't be coming out and maybe discover Henry. "I hope he doesn't decide to come out anyway," he said.

"William's bullheaded," Ma agreed, "But he's pretty careful about protecting his own hide. I don't think it'll be a problem."

Patrick looked at me with raised eyebrows at Ma's words. I struggled to keep a grin off my face. *Was Ma seeing through Bug-Eyes now? Was she having second thoughts?*

At suppertime, Ma rapped on my bedroom door to summon Henry to the table.

His gaunt, haggard face, reflecting the near starvation he had endured, peered around the door. "C—colored folks d—don't be eatin' with no w—white folks, ma'am," he stammered.

"Nonsense," Ma said sharply. "You've got to eat. We've got to eat. I'm not bringing you a tray every meal."

"I don't be meanin'—"

Ma interrupted him, her voice softer this time. "I know. But let's just eat. This is no time for standing on ceremony."

The next day after the noon meal, Henry would have gone back into my room after thanking Ma over and over again as he did after every meal, but she detained him. "Sit awhile, Henry," she said, "and tell us something about yourself."

Henry's eyes darted this way and that for a second, looking, I thought, like an animal caught and seeking escape. I held back a grin. It looked to me like Henry would as soon fight off the slave catchers as to sit and talk. But he did as Ma asked, although most of the time he kept his eyes on the floor.

He told us about his family, a light coming into his face as he spoke of his wife and three children—two boys, eight and ten, and a girl, six.

"Are they still in slavery?" Ma asked.

"Yes'm, they is. But hope they gets out soon. They's a woman fixin' to bring 'em north."

"This woman you speak of," Ma said, "she'll bring your family out through the Underground Railroad?"

"Not 'xactly. Sally, she be near white in color. Julia, too. The boys be black like me. Lady say she gonna dress up my Sally and Julia to look like a white lady and her little girl. The boys gonna be their slaves toting and fetching and such-like."

"I hope it works," Ma said quietly.

Patrick, who had taken up his usual stance by the window to watch for the slave catchers, turned to Henry and said, "How will you know where to meet? Canada's a big country."

Henry looked toward Patrick and again lowered his eyes so he seemed to be speaking to the floor. "Some Quaker folks seein' to that." He paused and wiped the back of his hand across his forehead. The afternoon was already hot and Henry's face glistened with sweat. I wondered if it was from nervousness, or the heat, or both. "I done fixed a name and a place in my head to be askin' for." He sat for a moment, his hands working in twisting, squeezing motions. When he spoke again, his voice had a husky sound as if he were close to tears. "Somethin' it go wrong and they don't never get to Canada, I tell them Quaker folk I be goin' back."

"You'd go back into slavery?" Patrick said. "Won't they retaliate in some way? Do something to you for running away?" he added, seeing the puzzled look on Henry's face.

"Could be they'd beat me some," Henry said. "It be a lesson they don't be soft on us. Don't spose they gonna kill me. Did old

Amos, though. But he got crippled when he got caught, so he no good to them. They use old Amos to scare us so's they think we's 'fraid to run. We is, but we runs anyways."

So caught up in Henry's story, I jumped and almost yelped when Patrick, still at the window, called out, "Dr. Isaac's coming."

Jackson, restless and bored with staying inside, had pushed a chair up beside Patrick, his nose pressed against the windowpane. Suddenly, with a little cry, he leaped from the chair. Patrick grabbed for him, but too late and the little boy, a flash of red hair and brown coveralls, was gone, the door standing open behind him as he ran up the road to meet Dr. Isaac.

Patrick turned a rueful grin toward us. "Dr. Isaac's brought us a dog," he said.

Chapter Thirteen

A Window to the World

"Come on girl," Jackson coaxed the big, golden-brown dog up the steps and into the house. "Come in and see everybody."

Dr. Isaac, bringing up the rear, grinned at Patrick and me standing inside the open doorway. Then his gaze shifted to Ma who was peering over my shoulder. "The more I thought about it," he said, "the more I was sure the dog was a good idea." Ivan Haskell says you can keep her, if she pleases you."

At Dr. Isaac's words, Jackson beamed at the dog. "Hear that?" he said. "You're going to be our dog. We'll have lots of fun. You'll like it here."

Inside the house, Patrick, with a quick grin at Jackson who was kneeling on the floor, his arms about the big dog's neck, asked what we were all wondering about. "Did you secure Henry a ticket on the Underground Railroad?"

"I sure did." Dr. Isaac turned to regard Henry, standing at the door of my room, an anxious look on his face. "They've a plan for you, but all I know is that someone is to pick you up at midnight out on what we call the old Plummer road. The man will be driving a wagonload of hay and whistling a tune like he has no cares in the world. When he goes by, you are to jump on the wagon and hide yourself in the hay." He turned to accept a hot cup of coffee from Ma, and after taking a cautious sip, explained to the rest of us that the pickup would take place at the bend in the road where the snag of a big dead tree has stood for years.

"Could I take him?" Patrick asked.

Dr. Isaac shook his head. "No, son. There's no sense in getting you any more involved. If I've been fooled and this is a setup and not the real Underground then they'll already know I'm guilty." He paused and looked around at all of us. "Of course, you will all be suspect, too. But with no proof..." He left the sentence unfinished and moved over to sit in Pa's chair where he began leafing through an old newspaper from the stack he'd brought out last week.

I helped Ma with supper while Patrick did the milking and split several armloads of wood to fill the wood box behind the stove.

After supper, Ma picked up her knitting and settled into her chair. Dr. Isaac went back to Pa's chair and picked up another newspaper, but after reading awhile dozed off, the newspaper falling to his lap. I got out an old ragged coat of Patrick's that Ma wanted me to rip up and cut in blocks for a heavy winter comforter. Patrick studied some law books that Dr. Isaac had bought from the widow of a lawyer. Jackson played with the new dog until darkness began to fall and Patrick had to put her outside to be our eyes and ears.

"If we leave her inside until dark," Dr. Isaac told us when he first brought the dog to us, "perhaps she will transfer her loyalties to this household." He smiled at Jackson who sat on the floor in front of the dog, her big head between his small hands, while he talked softly to her as if imparting lessons she would need to know. She in turn, responded with licks to his face. Turning back to smile at Ma, Dr. Isaac said, "It looks like it's working, too."

The night seemed to stretch out, each hour longer than the one before, and we all grew increasingly anxious. Dr. Isaac woke soon after falling asleep and he and Ma talked, their eyes straying often to the clock on the shelf above our table. I listened to them talk about Mrs. Haskell and the soon to arrive baby and about Mr. McDaniels having put his store up for sale. Again I wished I were grown so I could buy it from him and move to Burns Ferry so I would not have to live with Bug-Eyes.

When the clock's hands reached eleven, Dr. Isaac rose from his chair. "Well," he said. "It's time. It won't hurt to be a little early."

Ma had handed Henry a packet of food for his journey when a knock came at the door. We stood still as stones a second before scattering. Henry melted back into my room and Ma, remembering she was supposed to be sick, ran to her bed. I took up cutting quilt blocks again and Patrick picked up Jackson to pretend to be telling him a story. Dr. Isaac went to the door.

"Well, hello, Ivan," Dr. Isaac said, a bit too heartily, I thought. Then I half rose out my chair. *Why was Mr. Haskell here? Had he come for Dr. Isaac? Was Mrs. Haskell having her baby?*

Dr. Isaac stepped outside and closed the door behind him. "It's Mr. Haskell," I whispered to Ma, who was peering around the door of her room. "That's why the dog didn't bark."

In a few minutes Dr. Isaac was back inside leaving the door ajar. "It's Jane," he said, looking toward Ma. "The baby's not coming like it should. The midwife sent Ivan for me."

I gasped, cold shivers running through me. *Oh poor*

Johanna! I knew mothers and the babies, too, often died during childbirth and my heart sank like a stone.

"When I picked up the dog, I told him you were ill." Dr. Isaac spoke to Ma, now retying the apron she had flung aside when she'd hurried to her room. "But Ivan said he had to come anyway. He figured the immediate danger of losing his wife and baby outweighed the lesser risk of bringing back an illness to his family."

"Oh," Ma said. "I wish we could tell him the truth."

"Well, actually, I just now did," Dr. Isaac said, a smile briefly lighting his face. "He was so distraught. I told him you were feeling fine now. That I had made a mistake. I thought I could ease his mind that much, now that Henry will be on his way." He turned to Patrick. "I'm sorry, son, but you'll have to take him."

As Dr. Isaac bent to pick up his black bag, Ma said, "Could I go with you, Isaac?" Sudden tears sparkled in her eyes and as quickly she brushed them away. "I owe Jane Haskell a lot. She got me out of bed and going through the motions of living after James… after the letter." She turned to me. "Patrick shouldn't be gone long. Keep the door latched and we've got the sign still up. If you need to, bring the dog inside."

"We'll be all right," I said, drawing Jackson close for my own comfort. "You need to go, Ma."

As soon as the Haskell buggy pulled away taking Ma and Dr. Isaac, Patrick called Henry out of my room.

"If I could be knowing the way," Henry said. "No need you be risking…"

"No, Henry," Patrick interrupted, "I'm taking you. I know the way and time's getting short."

They started for the door. "Good luck, Henry," I said, just as the dog began to bark.

We froze, staring at the door and then at each other.

"What now?" Patrick muttered through clenched teeth.

We waited, listening to the dog's constant barking, our eyes going again and again to the clock as the minutes ticked by.

"It could be an animal," I whispered.

"Listen!" Patrick hissed. "She's growling now and coming closer. It sounds like something or someone is backing her up to the house. Henry!" He jerked around. But Henry had already disappeared into my room.

We heard the dog come up on the porch, still threatening whoever or whatever was out there with low snarling growls. I jumped about a foot when a deep voice called out, "Y'all in that there house! Call off your dog!"

My heart leaped up in my throat as I watched Patrick open the door a crack. "We've sick folks here," he called out. "I know it's too dark to see, but there's a quarantine sign on our door. The doctor put it there. It means we've got an illness that's catching. I'll call the dog in and set a candle out, if you want to come up and read it."

A harsh laugh answered Patrick. "Y'all wouldn't just be funnin' us now, would ya? We all's been a-watchin' and a-readin' sign. Saw your folks leave a while ago. Can't be no sickness, your folks off gallivantin'."

"Trying to fool us, ain't ya," another voice snarled. "Y'alls got that colored boy in there. Your fancy doctor sign's a hoax."

"There's two of them, like Henry said, " I whispered to no one in particular. *We all had ears, we all could tell that.*

"Come on, Zeke," The first voice growled again. "Let's flush the black bugger out."

"You come any closer and I'll sic the dog on you," Patrick warned.

"A little lead poisoning'll take care o' him."

At those words, Jackson, who had been watching big-eyed and silent, sprang for the door.

I grabbed the sleeve of his shirt and pulled him to me, clamping my arms tight around his small shoulders. "He won't shoot the dog," I whispered. *He might though.* I wasn't at all sure.

"Annie…" Jackson started to protest, but Patrick snapped at us to be quiet and reached for his gun from the rack by the door.

His action stunned me, and it was a moment before I realized that Jackson had ceased to struggle. "Let me go, Annie," he said. "I'll be good. Let me go."

As I dropped my arms, releasing Jackson, I glanced again at the clock. It was ten minutes until midnight. Ten minutes until the man would come for Henry. Suddenly I knew that if Henry were to get away, it would be up to me.

"I'm taking Henry out my bedroom window," I whispered to Jackson. "Tell Patrick so he can let those men in, if he has to. I grabbed his small chin tight in my hand, for I wanted him to know the seriousness of my next words. "If Patrick has to let them in, can you pretend to be awfully, awfully sick?"

"You bet!" Jackson's brows drew together in a frown and his little face took on such a determined look that I would have laughed had the situation not been so serious.

As I pushed open the door to my room, the lamplight behind me gave me a glimpse of one of Henry's legs disappearing out of my window. Certain to have realized we were all in grave danger, Henry must have decided to go alone. *I couldn't let him do that.* He'd never find the meeting place and would be captured for sure. I had never climbed out of a window in my life and with my long skirts I wasn't sure how to go about it. But I knew every second counted, so I ran to the window and putting my hands on the sill, heaved myself headfirst through the opening. I landed with a thud that, for a second, took my breath away.

"Miss?" Henry's anxious voice whispered out of the dark. "That you, Miss?"

"Yes," I answered. I jumped to my feet, a sudden rush of fear, now that I was out here in the dark, made me wish I'd let Henry manage on his own.

"You best be stayin', Miss," Henry said, offering me a way out. But I couldn't take it. I knew the way and he did not.

"Hurry," I whispered and started off toward the protection of the trees.

"Ah mercy," I heard Henry mutter as he followed after me. "I gonna be dead for sure, now."

His words puzzled me for a moment before I realized I, being a white girl, was adding to his danger. Now, if caught, he would not just be returned to slavery, but killed on the spot. They would act first and ask questions later, for they'd be certain he had kidnapped me. But, I told myself, defending my impulsive actions, time was short and I knew the way and he did not. It was a risk that, to me, had to be taken. But I was so scared I could hardly force myself to keep moving on through the trees.

With only a sliver of moon, the night was dark as ink. Tree branches reached like hands to grab at me, and once I stumbled over a rock or some other obstacle too dark to see. Our progress sounding overloud to my ears, I just knew the slave catchers were closing in on us, and remembering what Patrick said about slave catchers using dogs, and Dr. Isaac's words, "They could have picked up some by now," sent shivers along my spine.

A twig snapped underfoot and the shadowy form of an owl flew past on silent wings. Close by, so close it raised the hair on my scalp, something barked. I whipped around, visions of slave-hunting dogs leaped at us from the brush. *"What was that!"*

"A fox, Miss."

"Oh." I knew the bark of a fox. I'd heard it before. Just not on a dark night when I was running through the woods with a fugitive slave.

Again Henry insisted he go on alone, but I would not turn back. Without me, I was sure he would never meet up with the man on the wagonload of hay. Maybe, too, my stubbornness was a part of the knowledge that Henry had lived in my room, had jumped from my window. The window Pa had put in just for me. My window to the world. I hoped, with all my heart, it would prove to be Henry's window to freedom. It seemed a fitting legacy for my pa, and I wanted it to happen too much to turn back now.

When we reached the bend in the road where the wagonload of hay was to come for Henry, I whispered, "I know we're a little late. I hope he hasn't gone by."

"I hopes so, too, Miss." Henry's low, deep voice came to me out of the darkness. He had stepped back under the snag of dead tree, so, except for his voice, he might have been a part of the tree. "You be a gettin' on back, now. If the man don't be coming, I gonna head on north and keep a goin'."

Now I was as scared to go back as I was to stay with Henry. By now the slave catchers could have searched our house and be close on our trail. I had no doubt that Patrick, if he could, would be right after them, or maybe he was holding them at the house, his gun on them to give Henry time to get away. But they probably had guns, too. I had heard no gunshots, but still I was afraid to go back for fear that something might have happened to Patrick and Jackson. I was also afraid I would run into the slave catchers on the way back to the house. But I couldn't stay here either. If they found Henry with me, he would be killed. And if the wagon came, I'd still have to go back alone. If the wagon didn't come, Henry would go on, headed north, and I would still be alone. Cold shivers traveled along my spine, but I said as bravely as I could, "Well, good-bye and good luck, Henry."

He answered me, but no sign of him showed in the deep shadows of the tree. "Good-bye and luck go 'long wid you, Miss. It be powerful good you folks done me and I ain't gonna be forgettin' it none."

As I turned to go, I thought of Mr. Looney Barnes, the old man Johanna and I had met last fall on the trail. The old man who had had unexpected guests. Guests of color, I suspected. I wished he were here now to stay with Henry and take him, if the wagon didn't come, home to his smelly shack. Except, I thought with a half smile, the slave catchers could follow the trail of his smell.

Then the rock ledge popped into my head. If the wagon didn't come, Henry could hide there until the Underground could sneak him away. It would be the perfect hiding place. With water nearby and the packet of food Ma had given him, he could stay hidden for several days. By then, the slave catchers would surely give up and go on. It was a second before it hit me that Henry didn't know the way to the rock ledge and I would have to take him. My stomach lurched and fear crawled across my skin. *It was at least a half dozen miles from this bend in the road, and I'd have to come back alone in the dark. No, I just couldn't do it. But I had to, there was no other way.* Shivers of fear running through me, I squeezed my eyes tight and tried to gather courage, tried to will my fear away. I started to speak, to force the words about the rock ledge, past my stiff lips when a soft rustling sound in the trees and brush, close at hand, sent hysteria rising up in me like a rage of flood waters. Only my hands, clapped tight over my mouth, kept back my screams of terror. I stared, my feet rooted to the ground, and was stunned to see Patrick and Jackson step out of the trees. Like a sudden whoosh of wind, everything went right out of me and I fell to my knees and burst into tears.

Chapter Fourteen

The One-Armed Stranger

Johanna's little brother arrived early that next morning. "The poor little fellow was nearly worn out from fighting so hard to get born," Ma told us, a warm smile curving her lips. He's a beautiful child and much larger than expected." A twinkle sparkled in her eyes. "They named him Nathan Henry."

I stared at Ma. "How did they know about Henry?" I asked.

Ma grinned. "They didn't. I suggested Henry when they couldn't decide on a middle name." Her grin disappeared and left a solemn look. "I thought it was fitting as the child entered the world just as Henry was escaping into a new world of freedom... or so we hope."

The wagon never came for Henry that night, and Patrick, who knew of the rock ledge, had taken him there to await further instructions from the Underground. We never knew if Henry missed the wagon because we were late getting to the appointed place, or if, for some reason, the man and his wagon had not come by at all.

As Jackson and I hurried back toward home in the still dark, nearly moonless night, I jumped at every sound. Each time, I was certain we would come upon the slave catchers. A dozen times, in my mind, Jackson and I were captured and made to tell where Henry was, and it was with deep relief that we finally made it safely home. Patrick had put the dog in the house and she greeted us with happy barks and warm, wet licks to Jackson's face.

In the weeks that followed Henry's departure, we thought of him often. Dr. Isaac had contacted the Underground again, but we never heard, and probably never would hear, if he'd been spirited away and was now safe in Canada.

I still got the shivers remembering that night. After Henry and I had gone out my window, Patrick had allowed one of the men into the house. The swarthy pock-faced individual had needed only one look at Jackson lying in Ma's bed, to be convinced.

"The light was dim and with that raspberry jam he'd smeared on his face… his legs and arms twitching…" Patrick turned to Jackson, a grin matching the sparkle in his eyes. "What made you think of the jam?" he asked.

Puffed up with pride at his own cleverness, Jackson said, "I wanted to look catching."

"Well you certainly did," Patrick said, as he gave Jackson's red hair an affectionate tousling.

We took down the quarantine sign and gave it back to Dr. Isaac. A shame, I thought, that we couldn't keep it up forever and keep Bug-Eyes away. He came nearly every day now, riding his big, black thoroughbred horse, and as always was so perfectly groomed in a starched, white shirt, tan or black trousers, and polished leather boots to match.

Ma was always busy, of course, but took the time to sit with him. Today she had just finished scrubbing the floors. She left me to empty the pail of dirty water and hurried to sponge off her face and arms and tuck a few strands of dark hair back into the bun at the nape of her neck.

As Ma said it would be unseemly for her to entertain Bug-Eyes alone, either Patrick or I had to sit with them. Today, I was elected as Patrick was cleaning the chicken house. I told him he was lucky to have that nice smelly job. He just grinned at me. I stood a few minutes watching him shovel out the manure from under the roost, using up all the time I dared before Ma would come after me. I envied Jackson as he never had to sit with Ma and Bug-Eyes. He was off somewhere today with Girl, the dog Dr. Isaac had brought us the day the slave catchers came. The Haskells had called her Bessy, but Jackson always called her Girl and so that had become her name.

Settling down in a chair, I let go with a deep sigh, which earned me a quick reprimand in the form of a hard frown from Ma. Bug-Eyes, so full of himself, his pale fixed on Ma, probably didn't even notice.

I listened to their talk. Ma asked about Mr. McDaniels's store and for just a second something flickered across her face when Bug-Eyes told her it hadn't yet sold. What was it about Mr. McDaniels's store, I wondered, that put that odd expression on Ma's face?

As they talked, the drone of their voices made me sleepy, but I snapped out of my half-doze, wide awake, when Bug-Eyes said, "I don't mean to frighten you, Mary. And I've been wondering about even telling you, but…"

"But what, William?" Ma said.

"I met this fellow on the road today. He'd lost an arm somewhere. It'd been cut off at the elbow. The odd part is that he asked about you."

"About me?" Ma's eyebrows lifted in surprise.

"Yes. The children, too."

"Where did you meet him?" Ma asked.

"Back at the two mile corner. He rode up out of some trees and hailed me. At first I took him for an outlaw." Bug-Eyes paused, a frown darkening his face. "Perhaps he meant to rob me and when he found out I knew you, decided against it."

With a slight shake of her head, Ma said, "I just don't know who he could be."

"Well, he knows you, all right," Bug-Eyes said, his voice sharp edged, like in some way he doubted her.

Ma's cheeks colored. "What exactly did he say?" she asked.

"Just if I knew you. When I told him I did and quite well, too, he asked about your health and the children's, each by name." Bug-Eyes hesitated, clearing this throat. "I told him about your husband and the letter telling of his certain death, and that you and I were to be married next month." A frown wrinkled his brow. "He sure reacted odd to that news. I guess he hadn't heard about your husband. Without another word, he swung his horse, a big roan, around and rode back up into the trees."

"What color was that horse?" I leaned forward in my chair, the sudden rise of hope nearly suffocating me. *Did he say, roan? Could it have been Pa's Big Jake? Could it have been Pa?*

Bug-Eyes swung his head around to me. "Why?"

My face flushed with sudden anger. *Couldn't the man answer a simple question?* "I just want to know," I said through half-gritted teeth. "I thought you said a roan."

His bugged out eyes narrowed as he answered me. "I did. A barrel-chested blue roan."

I turned anxious eyes to Ma. She frowned and shook her head. "No, Annie. It can't be. I'm sure a lot of men have blue roan horses."

Bug-Eyes cocked his head and looked at Ma, a frown

darkening his face. "I seem to have been left out of this conversation," he said, "Am I to be enlightened or not?"

"I'm sorry, William," Ma said. "It's just that James rode a blue roan. Your mention of the man's horse startled Annie."

"I see," Bug-Eyes said. "Well, of course, that's nonsense."

Tears threatening to spill, I swallowed hard and sat back in my chair. I knew Ma was right, and although I hated to admit it, so was Bug Eyes. If the man had been our pa, he would have come right home. I knew that, but still the hope that somehow the one-armed man could be him struggled to live in my heart. After Bug-Eyes left, I hurried to find Patrick, hoping he would confirm my hope that somehow the man was Pa.

"He could be a slave catcher," Patrick said. "Remember those two men hunting Henry that night? He could be one of them. Only one man came in to see Jackson's very fine performance." His eyes twinkled a little at his memory of Jackson's jelly-smeared face and shaking, twitching tremors. "It could be they suspect we are associated with the Underground and think they can get the goods on us. Someone may even be offering cash money for information." He shrugged. "That's the best explanation I can give you, Annie. You know Pa would have come right on home." He grinned a slight, lopsided grin. "Especially since William told him he was marrying Ma."

I turned away to hide my tears.

Chapter Fifteen

A Change of Heart

My thirteenth birthday was on a Sunday and Ma invited Dr. Isaac and, of course, Bug-Eyes to dinner. Bug-Eyes didn't have to do anything but be himself to irritate me. But today he irritated me even more than usual. Every word that came out of his mouth, every expression on his face, made me want to scream. He was feeling especially jovial, a contrast from his usual humorless self, but still just as bigheaded and full of himself as always. He was acting more possessive of Ma, too. As if, I thought, he owned her already.

Ma had made my favorite meal—fried chicken, creamed potatoes, applesauce, green beans cooked with bacon, and a thickly frosted spice cake for my birthday cake. But for me it might just as well have all been sawdust, for my appetite vanished the minute we sat down at the table. Bug-Eyes, grinning his big, stupid grin, announced that soon his legs would be under our table everyday. He said "This table" not "Your table" and I thought, he doesn't yet dare to say "My table." "Today is Sunday, the 27th of July," he said. "One month and three days until our wedding," he added on a triumphant note.

Are we so stupid we don't know that? I wanted to say. *It was my birthday for goodness sakes.*

His big sappy grin still on his face when Ma, sitting next to him, passed him the potatoes, he closed his hands over hers a moment before taking the bowl from her, and his bug-eyes gleamed at her. *He had won the prize,* I thought. *My mother!*

Ma froze for an instant and her face flushed red. She ducked her head and a second later dropped her hands to her lap, wiping the backs of them on her Sunday apron.

Bug-Eyes just laughed.

My heart felt sick with dread. *One month and three days until the bars of our jail would fall in place.*

At the end of the meal, Ma brought out the spice cake she had baked for my birthday. As we handed our plates down to her for a slice of the frosted brown cake, Dr. Isaac said, smiling, "I suppose Annie's cinnamon spots made you decide on this flavor."

Ma smiled. "I hadn't thought of that. I made it because it's her favorite."

Bug-Eyes didn't know about Pa calling my freckles cinnamon spots. Of course he has to know everything, so Ma explained it to him.

He frowned and said with a little snort that sounded like contempt to me, "How fanciful. For a grown man, James seems to have been a little on the childish side."

A hot, blinding anger swept over me and before I knew quite what I was doing, I was on my feet glaring at Bug-Eyes and words were coming from my mouth. "You have no right to talk that way about Pa," I said. "You didn't know him. So you cannot judge him. I know you are my elder and it is disrespectful to talk to you this way, but you must earn the right to be respected, and, sir, making remarks about our pa is not being respectful." I stopped for a moment and felt a calmness come over me, a calmness that gave me added courage. "When you marry my mother," I said in a level voice, "you must never, ever say anything but good about our pa, or… or… I will run away from home." I paused again and gulped in a deep breath of air before adding, "And I will take Ma and Jackson with me. We'll run away and go find Patrick and live with him."

Sudden tears flooded my eyes and choked off any further words and I stood there trembling, partly ashamed at my outburst, but triumphant, too, for I had meant every word. Patrick rose and pulled me into his arms. My head buried deep in Patrick's shoulder, I heard Bug-Eyes say, cold as ice, "Mary, are you going to let her get away with that?"

"Yes, William," Ma said, "I believe I am." I heard her chair scrape the floor as she pushed it back and stood up. "Why don't you come outside with me for a minute," she said.

Patrick sat me back down in my chair as Bug-Eyes followed Ma outside, the door closing softly behind them.

I pushed my slice of birthday cake aside and turned to Dr. Isaac, my wet cheeks burned with embarrassment. "I shouldn't have said that. It was rude of me."

"It was something that rather needed saying," Dr. Isaac said solemnly. "Sometimes a person has to speak up. It should have been me, though. I should have talked to your mother. I should have asked her if she really wanted to marry William, or if she had other reasons, besides love and affection, for accepting his proposal."

"She wants me to study law," Patrick said. "If she married again, I'd be free to go. And I wanted that, I'm ashamed to say."

Dr. Isaac nodded. "That only means you're normal, son… human. You have a need, too. But if she's marrying him to let you go, well, we can work out something, don't you think?" He was silent for a moment. When he spoke again, his words came out slowly, as if choosing them carefully. "Sometimes, we're afraid to question another's judgment. Fear that we'll lose the affection of the one we love keeps us from taking the chance. But maybe we should take that chance anyway." He smiled a soft smile and reached for my hand. "You did no wrong, my dear. He was being disrespectful to your pa's memory and it hurt you and you spoke your piece, which sometimes, and in this case, seems to have been the best course of action." He looked thoughtful a moment and then added," At least it's out in the open now, so perhaps we can talk about it with your ma."

Jackson, who had listened wordlessly to our talk, scooted from his chair and came around to look up at me, his little face serious. "I don't like him, either, Annie. When Ma's not looking, he talks mean to me, and Girl growls if he comes too close to me."

I hugged my little brother, struggling to hold back a fresh rush of tears. Looking over his head, I saw Ma open the door and step inside. Hope flooded my heart, for she was alone.

Her eyes searched our faces a minute before she spoke, and it was with relief and joy that I heard her words. "William and I have come to the conclusion that we are not well suited to each other." I watched a smile start on her lips and grow to shine from her blue eyes. "So," she added, "we are not getting married after all."

Through the sudden surge of happiness, came a little whisper of doubt to nag at me. "Was it because of what I said?"

Ma laughed. A merry, chuckling sound. "Yes, it was because of what you said, Annie, dear. You said what I should have been able to see a long time ago. And actually I did, but he represented security for us all." She paused and looked at Patrick. "I knew you could go to Pittsburgh." She raised her hand to

Patrick's protest, silencing him, and turned to look at Jackson and me. "I did worry about both of you, but I know you are both strong, independent…" She smiled a soft little smile. "I hoped my love would see you through until you both could leave home." She raised a corner of her apron, covering her good dress, and wiped at her eyes before adding, "It was a fool notion."

Eyes glistening, she turned to Dr. Isaac. "Do you think I did the right thing?"

A smile lit up his face and, getting up from his chair, he drew her into his arms. "I would say so, my dear," he said, and kissed the top of her head.

Ma stayed in his arms a moment before stepping back and looking up at him. "Do you know if Mr. McDaniels's store is still for sale?" Her voice had changed, so her words came out small and weak.

"I believe it is." A puzzled look grew on Dr. Isaac's face. "Why do you ask, Mary?"

"Because…" She seemed to be studying the floor, her hands jammed deep in her apron pockets.

"Yes, Mary?" Dr. Isaac's fingertips lifted her chin until she looked up at him.

"Because." She drew a deep breath. "I'm going to try and sell this farm and use the money to buy his store." She looked at Patrick. "It'll take awhile, but Annie can help with the store and then you can go on with your plans." She hesitated a moment, and her cheeks flushed red. "But if it's to work out, you and Annie will have to teach me to cipher figures and read a little."

Positively giddy with happiness, I clapped my hands and twirled around to look at Patrick. A wide grin covered his face as he assured Ma we would both be delighted to teach her to read and write and do numbers.

That night in my bed, lying flat on my back, I looked toward the outline of my window and whispered to Pa. "I wish you could come home, but I know you can't. We'll leave here, Pa, and I will miss this window—my window to the world. I will love and miss you forever, but I will be happy, too." Then I turned on my side and sleep soon claimed me.

Within a week, Ma had sold the farm and had agreed on a price with a surprised and pleased Mr. McDaniels for his store and post office. I was thrilled, and felt as if my feet hardly touched the ground. But I dared not hope too much until the price was settled and the agreement made. But when that was done, I let go of my fears and let my gaze wander from shelf to shelf, all filled with such a variety of goods, from spices to candles to bolts of calico and leather shoes. On the floor were barrels of crackers and pickles and apples and leaning against the wall nearest the door, sacks of potatoes, onions, and beans. Everything in the store gave off such a wonderful, blended smell. I breathed deeply, imagining myself behind the counter, a stub of a pencil in my hand as I figured my customer's purchases. Then I would put my pencil behind my right ear as Mr. McDaniels always did, hand over the purchases, and turn my smile to the next customer.

One day, at home, I took one of Patrick's well-used pencils and nestled it behind my ear for practice. Mr. McDaniels's nearly bald head had made it easy to find the pencil again, but I decided I would have to start wearing my hair pulled back, like Ma did, so the pencil wouldn't get lost in my thick, curly hair.

Oh, but I was so excited, I felt at times as if I would burst before the day came when we would actually be working in the store.

Yet sadness followed me, too. And sometimes the sadness seemed as overwhelming as my happiness. I hated to have to sell off the cows, especially stubborn old Blossom, and the chickens, cackling and pecking in the barnyard. Even the pigs, grunting and rooting and squealing, seemed precious to me now. I cried the day the last of our livestock was sold, leaving only Nick and Ned.

Eventually Ma would sell the big workhorses, too, and buy a small, single-horse buggy, but for now she was keeping them and the big wagon.

The day Ma had Patrick drive her to Burns Ferry and meet with Mr. McDaniels for the last time, I begged off going. This one last day I wanted to spend with Johanna, for months might pass before we would see each other again. After some argument, Ma had relented and let me stay home, since Girl would be here. Runaway slaves and "one-armed" slave catchers had made Ma a lot more cautious, and me as well.

"You take the dog along with you to Johanna's," Ma reminded me as Patrick helped her up into the wagon. In the pale light of dawn, her bonnet cast shadows across her face.

"I will, Ma," I said. "Don't worry, I'll be fine."

There was very little work left to do, as Ma and I had scoured and scrubbed the house clean for the new owners. After I did up our breakfast dishes, I went into my room and started putting my things in a crate to take to our new home behind the store in Burns Ferry.

Finished with that I sat on my bed. Girl put her big head up on my lap and as I petted her, I looked at my window and a few tears leaked from my eyes. My new room had a window, but not one Pa had put in just for me. I thought again of the night Henry had escaped through my window and I wondered where he was now. That made me think of the old man and his unexpected guests, whoever they might have been. A little grin chased away my tears. One would have to be desperate to stand the odor he carried on his person, not to mention the shack where he lived. Dr. Isaac had said it smelled as bad or worse than something dead. But, remembering Henry, I knew those people were desperate—willing to take the chance of losing everything, even life itself, to be free. Bad smells would be the least of their problems.

With a sigh, I rose to my feet. It was time to go to Johanna's. At the door, I looked back at my window and the memory of the night I had tumbled through it headfirst brought a grin to my face. I decided to climb out of it again, this time using my feet instead of my head. I wasn't quite tall enough to stand on the floor and lift my legs up over the sill, so I ran and got the little stool that Pa had made one Christmas for Ma. That made it easy to get my legs up and over the sill to dangle down outside. The window was too low for me to sit up straight and I had to tilt my body back as I slid out and down to the ground. I landed solidly on my feet. Hearing Girl whine, I looked up to see her peering out at me. She was up on her hind legs, her front paws on the windowsill. "Come on, Girl. Jump!" I called. She disappeared from sight and I was about to go around to the door for her when her big golden-brown body hurled through the window. Squatting down, I hugged her and told her what a good dog she was. In return, she licked my face. As I started off toward the trees, she followed, padding softly behind me.

Chapter Sixteen

Pa

The morning breeze was pleasantly soft on my face as I climbed up through the trees to the top of a small knoll where I could look down on the farm below. I stood a while, remembering. I could almost see Pa coming up from the barn, Ma on her knees in the garden pulling carrots for supper, and Patrick and Jackson, poles over their shoulders, headed for the creek where the fish lurked in watery shadows. In my mind, I saw how the oak tree by the front door changed with the seasons, from full and green, as it was now, to bronze, and then to bare dark branches, sometimes topped with snow. I had lived on this farm for half of my life, and I thought I would remember it always. But would I? Would other places become as dear to me, and would the memories I now had of this place unravel over the years? Suddenly filled with a sadness even tears could not dispel, I turned away and started back through the trees, anxious now to see Johanna and her family. I hoped little Nathan Henry would be awake while I was there. He was such a happy baby, cooing and smiling. Just thinking of him was already lifting my spirits.

As I angled off down the hill and entered the stand of red maples Henry had staggered out of that day in June, Girl's ears lifted and the hair along her backbone bristled. She slowed, taking cautious steps, a low growl coming from deep in her throat.

"What is it, Girl?" I whispered.

With a sudden, loud bark, she raced off through the trees, heading towards the little cemetery where the twins were buried.

I stood still, listening. But all I could hear above the beating of my heart were the flute-like tones of a wood thrush, the flutter of leaves stirred by the soft summer wind, and Girl's loud barking. Then, abruptly, there was silence. I could no longer hear Girl, the wood thrush had ceased its singing, and even the pleasant little breeze had died away and the fluttering leaves hung still. Slowly, my heartbeat returned to normal. Whatever Girl had heard, some animal, I supposed, must have run off. The dog was probably now sniffing every bush and tree trying to pick up a scent. At any minute I expected to see her big, golden-brown body dash toward me. The chase over, she would walk with me until some other scent or sight sent her off again. But after walking a few hundred feet and still no sign of her, I grew uneasy and my footsteps slowed. My eyes and ears searched for any sight or sound and my heart began a slow little hammering in my chest.

I walked a few more steps and a soft sound, too low to determine what it was, came to my ears and I strained to hear the sound again. *What was it?* It had sounded like a voice.

Step by cautious step, I moved through the trees, placing my feet softly, carefully, my hands catching and easing aside each branch, each twig, so I made as little sound as possible. *Where was that dog! That Girl!*

The sound came again, clearer. *It was a voice! A man's voice deep and somehow familiar.*

"Old Towser's gone on I expect, and that's why they've got you."

It was like running into a wall. *I knew that voice! It was Pa's!*

I burst from the trees, soundlessly calling his name, my throat too full for words. And there he was! He was standing by the little fenced-in cemetery with Girl beside him.

He looked up and his face, above his thick red-brown beard, paled. I stared at him, rooted to the spot of ground I stood on. He came to me in long, swift strides. I fell against him and he held me tight, whispering soft, groaning words. "Annie... Dear, dear, Annie."

Sobbing and shaking, as if with the ague, I drew back, and through my watery vision looked up into my pa's dear, familiar face. "Oh, Pa," I cried hiccupping every word, "we thought you were dead. We got a letter..."

"I know." His voice was a hoarse, strangled sound.

"Mr. Snell saw you," I wiped my wet eyes and runny nose on the sleeve of my dress. "But he didn't know it was you. Why didn't you come home, Pa?" It was then I remembered and my eyes moved from his face to his right arm. From the elbow down his arm was gone. A deep swell of tenderness welled up and filled my heart. I touched the sleeve tied with a leather string at the elbow. "Is that why, Pa? Did you think that would make a difference to us?"

Pa sighed. "I'll try to explain, Annie," he said. He motioned me to sit on a grassy patch of ground and sat down beside me, stretching out his legs. Taking my right hand in his left one, he gripped it firmly, but gently. Girl lay down at an angle next to me and put her head on my lap, her amber-colored eyes on Pa's face. I couldn't help but smile at her, for it was as if she, too, wanted to hear Pa's story.

"Mr. Snell told me you got the letter from Richards." Pa began.

I nodded.

"Well, when I left Richards in camp that day, I was still sick, dizzy as all get out. But we needed fresh meat—our rations were all but gone, and Richards was too sick to go. Besides," he added, with a small grin, "he's a terrible shot."

Girl stretched until her warm wet tongue could lick at the little she could reach of my hand in Pa's. "And then what?" I said.

"Big Jake and I surprised an old she-bear with cubs. We must have been upwind, and she didn't smell us, or Jake, her, until too late. If I hadn't felt so rotten, I'd have been more alert and might have avoided her. She came at us, on attack, and Big Jake bolted, unseating me on the first jump. My boot caught in the stirrup and I bounced along the ground for a ways. By the time Big Jake calmed down, I was about skinned raw and my arm was broken, the bone pushed through the skin. "I was lucky, though. Not more'n and hour later a trapper and his Indian wife found me and took me back up into the mountains to their cabin."

"They took Big Jake in too, I guess," I said and looked over at Pa's horse moving along slowly, cropping grass, his bridle reins dragging the ground. "What happened to Patrick's horse?"

"I don't know." Pa sighed heavily. "I left him in camp with Richards. I suppose he's in California somewhere."

I frowned and glanced down at the sleeve tied off with a leather string. "Did they call a doctor to do that?"

"No. There are no doctors in the mountains. They did it

themselves. It was too badly infected to save. They had to cut it off, or let me die."

I winced, imagining the pain. "It must have hurt a lot," I said.

A small smile touched Pa's lips. "Actually, I was delirious at the time. Completely out of my head, so I don't recall feeling a thing." He paused and added, a little twist to his lips, "It sure was sore afterwards, though, and the medicine they gave me, steeped from the bark of some tree or weed, tasted awful." He grinned a wry little grin. "It's a wonder their medicine didn't kill me."

I barely heard his little attempt at lightness. "Did you go on to California after you got well?" I asked.

Pa's face sobered. "By the time I was well enough to travel, winter had set in, so I stayed with my benefactors until spring. I scrawled a pretty sorry looking letter to your mother and sent it with a friend of theirs, a trapper called Bobcat Charley who winters down at Fort Bridger. He was to send it out from the fort, although I knew by then it might not go before spring."

"We never got it," I said.

"I know that now, but not then. When spring came, I headed for California, but my heart wasn't in it. One morning I woke knowing I had to go home. On the way back, I stopped at Fort Bridger to get another horse to spell Big Jake, and found out that Bobcat Charley hadn't shown up last fall."

"What happened to him?" I asked.

Pa shrugged. "Who knows? He might have met with an accident or taken ill. Or he might have taken a notion to spend the winter in an Indian camp. I just don't know."

"So you were coming home," I said. "You'd given up on striking it rich."

He smiled, looking suddenly bashful. "You might say I saw the tail of the elephant, I was that close. But I had finally figured out that some things are more important than gold."

A warm glow flooded through me. To see the elephant, I knew, was a saying often used about going to California. So, because of us, Pa had come back before seeing the whole elephant, before even getting to California. "We were more important than gold," I said.

.   "Yes. You and your brothers and your mother." He sobered, sadness lodging in his brown eyes.

"Then why didn't you come home after you got here? After you saw Mr. Snell?"

He ducked his head and spoke without looking at me. "One night I dreamed that Jackson died." He turned his head, his eyes seeking mine. "Before I met Luke and Spotted Fawn, the trapper and his wife, I would have scoffed at dreams meaning anything, but Spotted Fawn said she often sees things in dreams. She said she dreamed of me the night before they found me."

"Jackson was awfully sick for a while," I said. "but even if he had died, I still don't know why you couldn't come home."

Pa looked toward the small graveyard. "It's my fault those babies died. Your mother asked me to wait until after their second birthdays. I wouldn't wait that long. She almost never forgave me and I was afraid if Jackson... If any of you..." He coughed and tried again. "I had to know before I faced your mother." He smiled a hard bitter smile. "That's why I stopped Mr. Snell to ask if you were all well. I saw he was a stranger, but I hoped he would know you." He paused and grinned a crooked grin that never reached his eyes. "I never dreamed how well. After talking to him and finding out I was dead to all of you, the marriage date was set, and, the man, judging by his clothes and the horse he rode, quite prosperous, I decided it would be best for all of you if I stayed dead."

"You... you weren't coming home at all?" Quick anger brought a rush of hot tears. I blinked them away as I jerked my hand from Pa's and jumped to my feet. Glaring down at him, I said, "You would let us believe you were dead! You would let us suffer the pain of your death, forever?"

"I know it's hard for you to understand." He got to his feet and turned from me, from my anger. His eyes followed the blue roan, still cropping grass. When he spoke again his words were broken sounding, and at first, he stammered. "You—you—you see… That Mr. Snell… He—he was all I wasn't… Could never be. It was plain he had money—his clothes looked to be made of the best of linens and wools, his horse, a fine blooded animal. I knew I was looking at a well-to-do man who could offer your mother so much more than I could." He turned back to me and his eyes were deep wells of sorrow. "I… I had nothing. No gold. Not even two arms. How well was I going to farm with one arm?"

"So you hid from us," I said, my anger dissolving in the face of his obvious suffering.

"Yes. There's a rock shelter some four or five miles back. It has good grass and water."

"Oh," I said. I started to tell him I knew about the rock ledge, but that would lead to telling about Blossom and Henry, and even that we had met old Mr. Looney Barnes, and all that could wait. Now I needed to know how long Pa had spied on us. How long he had deliberately deceived us into thinking he was dead. "So you spied on us," I said and the anger came back to me again, but not so intense, the fierceness tamed by the shadow of sorrow in his eyes.

"Yes. I came every day, fighting with myself each time about giving you all up so you could have a better life than I would ever be able to give you." He shook his head and turned from me again, but not before I saw the shiny mist of tears in his eyes. For what seemed many moments, he was silent, his gaze fastened on some distant point beyond us.

I waited. The wood thrush sang again and a red bird flashed a thread of color through the trees. The sun was climbing toward midday and Girl, who had wandered off a few minutes before, returned and nuzzled my hand.

Finally Pa spoke. "Today was to be my last day. One last glimpse of all of you before I left forever. But I saw the wagon leave. I thought you were all in it, and I thought, well, I'll wait until they come back, and then I'll go. He looked at me and a small smile that looked wrapped in pain crossed his face. "I didn't realize you hadn't gone, too."

A new surge of anger caught me off guard and I forgot Pa's pain and felt only my own hot rage, my own suffering. "So you were going to let us believe you were dead?" Tears trembled on my lashes a moment and then fell drop by drop. "Sorry I spoiled your plans, Pa. Now you'll have to come home."

"I know." Pa's face and voice sagged as if with weariness. "But I can offer your mother a divorce so she can marry her Mr. Snell."

Suddenly it dawned on me that I'd not told Pa about Mr. Snell and Ma, and a laugh, crazy sounding in my ears, bubbled out of me. "Oh, Pa," I said. "Ma's not going to marry Mr. Snell. She changed her mind. She was just going to do it so Patrick could go to Pittsburgh and study law." I laughed again at the bewilderment mixed with hope I saw in Pa's eyes. I reached for his hand, threading my fingers through his. "And guess what, Pa? Patrick will soon be going away to study law. Ma sold the farm and bought Mr. McDaniels's store. She says in a year or two she and I can run it alone, so Patrick will be free to go. And now…" I swung our clasped hands merrily back and forth,

"Now you are here, so Patrick won't even have to wait at all."

"Well, I'll be," Pa said, sounding stunned and bewildered, like he'd just wakened from a fevered sleep. "So that's why the livestock's gone. I thought you must be moving to Mr. Snell's place."

"Nope," I said, grinning wide with happiness. "And guess what?" I heard my voice puff up with pride. "Patrick and I are teaching Ma to read and cipher figures. She's catching on terribly fast, too."

An odd looked crossed Pa's face. "I'm happy for her," he said, but his voice didn't sound happy. It sounded scared.

I looked at him, puzzled by his reaction. A small, yellow butterfly fluttered through the air and landed on the fence that enclosed the twins' grave site. I looked up at Pa and frowned to hide the fear welling up inside me. "You sound like you don't want to come home. You are coming home, aren't you?"

"Yes, Annie." He nodded his head and his eyes looking into mine grew shadowed and hid whatever feelings lay there. "Yes. But I don't think your ma is going to be too pleased to see me. It sounds like she doesn't need me at all. I g—guess..." he stammered a little, stopped and repeated himself. "I guess she's quite capable of managing all by herself."

I considered his words. What he said was true. Ma could manage all by herself. But I knew she had once loved Pa. Her grief had been too deep, too lasting, for her love to have vanished so soon. No, I was sure Ma would welcome him back with open arms. She might be mad at him for a while, but she wouldn't stay mad. Mostly she'd be angry with him for making her suffer so long and so hard, but after that, she would forgive him and let him back into her heart.

A vision of Henry, sitting in our house, came to me and I remembered the emotion in his voice as he told us he would go back into slavery to be with his family. For them, he would give up his freedom, risk harsh punishment, or whatever else it took. But he had to know, too, that back in the slave owner's hands, they could each be sold to different masters and never see each other again. That made me think of Ma, who would marry Mr. Snell to let Patrick go free, and then, with a brimming heart full of love for Pa, I thought of his intended sacrifice, his "fool notion" as Ma would call it, that we would be better off with Mr. Snell than with him.

A wave of pure joy washed over me and I laughed at the idea that me, still just a girl, could see things more clearly than Pa could, at least for this moment. I thought of explaining to him that I knew that love, honest and true, ran too deep in the heart to be turned off or on at will. But just as quickly, I decided I would let him find that all out for himself. Perhaps there was still some anger at him, too, for I thought with a kind of satisfaction, *It will serve him right to suffer a little while longer.* With a laugh, I turned to him. "Come on, Pa. Let's go home. Your Indian friend isn't the only one who dreams dreams that come true."

Pa gave me a quick look, and for a second the scared anxious expression on his face lifted. "What did you dream?" he asked.

I laughed again and answered, "That I was riding behind you on Big Jake, and we were happy again." I grabbed his hand and tugging on it turned toward his blue roan horse. "Come on," I cried gaily, "let's make my dream come true."